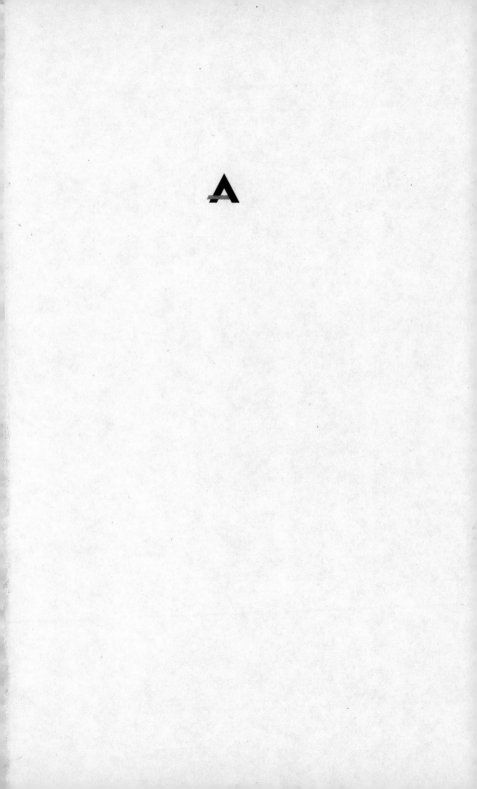

High Lonesome

High Lonesome

Barry Hannah

The Atlantic Monthly Press
New York

The following stories were previously published elsewhere: "Drummer Down,"
Southern Review; "The Agony of T. Bandini," *Gulf Coast;* "Uncle High
Lonesome," *Men Without Ties;* "Snerd and Niggero," "Repulsed,"
The Quarterly; "Get Some Young," *Reckon;* "Taste Like a Sword,"
The Oxford American; "Two Gone Over," *Esquire;* "A Creature in the
Bay of St. Louis," *Sports Afield;* "The Ice Storm," *Outside.*

Published simultaneously in Canada
Printed in the United States of America

FIRST EDITION

Library of Congress Cataloging-in-Publication Data
Hannah, Barry.
    High lonesome / Barry Hannah. — 1st ed.
        p.   cm.
    ISBN 0-87113-668-6
    1. United States—Social life and customs—20th century—Fiction.
I. Title.
PS3558.A476H54   1996
813'.54—DC20   96-30316

Design by Laura Hammond Hough

The Atlantic Monthly Press
841 Broadway
New York, NY 10003
10 9 8 7 6 5 4 3 2 1

For Richard and Lisa Howorth

HEAVEN IS PALS

Contents

Get Some Young

SINCE HE HAD RETURNED FROM KOREA he and his wife lived in mutual disregard, which turned three times a month into animal passion then diminished on the sharp incline to hatred, at last collecting in time into silent equal fatigue. His face was ordinarily rimmed with a short white beard and his lips frozen like those of a perch, such a face as you see in shut-ins and winos. But he did not drink much anymore, he simply often forgot his face as he did that of his wife in the blue house behind his store. He felt clever in his beard and believed that his true expressions were hidden.

Years ago when he was a leader of the Scouts he had cut way down on his drink. It seemed he could not lead the Scouts without going through their outings almost full drunk. He would get too angry at particular boys. Then in a hollow while they ran ahead planting pine trees one afternoon he was thrust by his upper bosom into heavy painful sobs. He could not stand them anymore and he quit the Scouts and the bonded whiskey at the same time. Now and then he would snatch a dram and return to such ecstasy as was painful and barbed with sorrow when it left.

This man Tuck last year stood behind the counter heedless of his forty-first birthday when two lazy white girls came in and raised their T-shirts then ran away. He worried they had mocked him in his own store and only in a smaller way was he certain he was still desirable and they could not help it, minxes. But at last he was more aggrieved over this than usual and he felt stuffed as with hot meat breaking forth unsewed at the seams. Yes girls, but through his life he had been stricken by young men too and became ruinously angry at them for teasing him with their existence. It was not clear whether he wished to ingest them or exterminate them or yet again, wear their bodies as a younger self, all former prospects delivered to him again. They would come in his life and then suddenly leave, would they, would they now? Particular Scouts, three of them, had seemed to know their own charms very well and worked him like a gasping servant in their behalf. Or so it had felt, mad wrath at the last, the whiskey put behind him.

The five boys played in the Mendenhall pool room for a few hours, very seriously, like international sportsmen in a castle over a bog, then they went out on the sidewalks mimicking the denizens of this gritty burg who stood and ambled about like escaped cattle terrified of sudden movements from any quarter. The boys were from the large city some miles north. When they failed at buying beer even with the big hairy Walthall acting like Peter Gunn they didn't much care anyway because they had the peach wine set by growing more alcoholic per second. Still, they smoked and a couple of them swore long histrionic oaths in order to shake up a meek druggist. Then they got in the blue Chevrolet Bel Air and drove toward their camp on the beach of the Strong River. They had big hearts and somehow even more confidence because there were guns in the car. They hoped some big-nosed crimp-eyed seed would follow them but none did. Before the bridge road took them to the water they stopped at the store for their legitimate country food. They had been here many times but they were all some bigger now. They did not know the name of the man in there and did not want to know it.

Bean, Arden Pal, Lester Silk, Walthall, and Swanly were famous to one another. None of them had any particular money or any special girl. Swanly, the last in the store, was almost too good-looking, like a Dutch angel, and the others felt they were handsome too in his company as the owner of a pet of great beauty might feel, smug in his association. But Swanly was not vain and moved easily about, graceful as a tennis player from the era of Woodrow Wilson, though he had never played the game.

From behind the cash register on his barstool Tuck from his hidden whitened fuzzy face watched Swanly without pause. On his fourth turn up the aisle Swanly noticed this again and knew certainly there was something wrong.

Mister, you think I'd steal from you?

What are you talking about?

You taking a picture of me?

I was noticing you've grown some from last summer.

You'd better give me some cigarettes now so we can stamp that out.

The other boys giggled.

I'm just a friendly man in a friendly store, said Tuck.

The smothered joy of hearing this kept the rest of them shaking the whole remaining twenty minutes they roamed the aisles. They got Viennas, sardines, Pall Malls, Winstons, Roi-Tans, raisins; tamales in the can, chili and beans, peanut butter, hoop and rat cheese, bologna, salami, white bread, mustard, mayonnaise, Nehi, root beer, Orange Crush; carrots, potatoes, celery, sirloin, Beech-Nut, a trotline, chicken livers, chocolate and vanilla Moon Pies, four pairs of hunting socks, batteries, kitchen matches. On the porch Swanly gave Walthall the cigarettes because he did not smoke.

Swanly was a prescient boy. He hated that their youth might end. He saw the foul gloom of job and woman ahead, all the toting and fetching, all the counting of diminished joys like sheep with plague; the arrival of beard hair, headaches, the numerous hospital trips, the taxes owed and the further debts, the mean and ungrateful children, the washed and waxen dead grown thin and like bad fish heaved into the outer dark. He had felt his own beauty drawn from him in the first eruption of sperm, an accident in the bed of an aunt by marriage whose smell of gardenia remained wild and deep in the pillow. Swanly went about angry and frightened and much saddened him.

Walthall lived on some acreage out from the city on a farm going quarter speed with peach and pecan trees and a few head of cattle. Already he had made his own peach brandy. Already he had played viola with high seriousness. Already he had been deep with a "woman" in Nashville and he wrote poems about her in the manner of E. A. Poe at his least in bonging rhymes. In every poem he expired in some way and he wanted the "woman" to watch this. Already he could have a small beard if he wanted, and he did, and he wanted a beret too. He had found while visiting relatives around the community of Rodney a bound flock of letters in an abandoned house, highly erotic missiles cast forth by a swooning inmate of Whitfield, the state asylum, to whatever zestfully obliging woman once lived there. These he would read to the others once they were outside town limits and then put solemnly away in a satchel where he also kept his poetry. A year ago Walthall was in a college play, a small atmospheric part but requiring much dramatic amplitude even on the streets thereafter. Walthall bought an ancient Jaguar sedan for nothing, and when it ran, smelling like Britain on the skids or the glove of a soiled duke, Walthall sat in it aggressive in his leisure as he drove about subdivisions at night looking in windows for naked people. Walthall was large but not athletic and his best piece of acting was collapsing altogether as if struck by a deer rifle from somewhere. For Walthall reckoned he had many enemies, many more than even knew of his existence.

Swanly was at some odds with Walthall's style. He would not be instructed in ways of the adult world, he did not like talking sex. Swanly was cowlicked and blithe in his boy ways and he meant to stay that way. He was hesitant even to learn new words. Of all the boys. Swanly most feared and loathed Negroes. He had watched the Negro young precocious in their cursing and dancing and he abhorred this. The only role he saw fit in maturity was that of a blond German cavalry captain. Among Walthall's recondite possessions, he coveted only the German gear from both world wars. Swanly would practice with a monocle and cigarette and swagger stick. It was not that he opposed those of alien races so much but that he aspired to the ideal of the Nordic horseman with silver spurs whom he had never seen. The voices of Nat King Cole and Johnny Mathis pleased him greatly. On the other hand he was careful never to eat certain foods he viewed as negroid, such as Raisinets at the movies. There was a special earnest purity about him.

The boys had been to Florida two years ago in the 1954 Bel Air owned by the brother of Arden Pal. They were stopped in Perry by a kind patrolman who thought they looked like runaway youth. But his phone call to Pal's home put it right. They went rightly on their way to the sea but for a while everybody but Swanly was depressed they were taken for children. It took them many cigarettes and filthy songs to get their confidence back. Uh found your high school ring in muh baby's twat, sang Walthall with the radio. You are muh cuntshine, muh only cuntshine, they sang to another tune. From shore to shore AM teenage castrati sang about this angel or that, chapels and heaven. It was a most spiritual time. But Swanly stared fixedly out the window at the encroaching palms, disputing the sunset with his beauty, his blond hair a crown over his forehead. He felt bred out of a golden mare with a saber in his hand, hair shocked back in stride with the wind. Other days he felt ugly, out of an ass, and the loud and vulgar world too soon pinched his face.

The little river rushed between the milky bluffs like cola. Pal dug into a clay bank for a sleeping grotto, his tarp over it. He placed three pictures of draped bohemian women from the magazine *Esquire* on the hard clay walls and under them he placed his flute case, pistol, and Mossberg carbine with telescope mounted there beside two candles in holes, depicting high adventure and desire, the grave necessities of men.

The short one called Lester Silk was newly arrived to the group. He was the veteran army brat of several far-flung bases. Now his retired father was going to seed through smoke and ceaseless hoisting on his own petard of Falstaff beers. Silk knew much of weapons and spoke often of those of the strange sex, men and women, who had preyed the perimeters of his youth. These stories were vile and wonderful to the others yet all the while they felt that Silk carried death in him in some old way. He was not nice. Others recalled him as only the short boy, big nose and fixed leer—nothing else. His beard was well on and he seemed ten years beyond the rest.

Bean's father, a salesman, had fallen asleep on a highway cut through a bayou and driven off into the water. The police called from Louisiana that night. All of the boys were at the funeral. Right after it Bean took his shotgun out hunting meadowlarks. The daughter of his maid was at the house with her mother helping with the funeral buffet. She was Bean's age. She told Bean it didn't seem nice him going hunting directly after his father's funeral. He told her she was only a darkie and to shut up, he made all the rules now. Her feelings were hurt and her mother hugged her, crying, as they watched young Bean go off over the hill to the pine meadows with his chubby black mutt Spike. Bean was very thin now. He had a bad complexion. He ran not on any team but only around town and the gravel roads through the woods. Almost every hour out of school he ran, looking ahead in forlorn agony and saying nothing to anybody. He was The Runner, the boy with a grim frown. When he ran he had wicked ideas on girls. They were always slaves and hostages. His word could free them or cause them to go against all things sacred. Or he would leave them. Don't leave, don't leave. I'll do anything. But I must go. After the death of his father he began going to the police station when he was through with his run. He begged to go along on a call. He hoped somebody would be shot. He wished he lived in a larger city where there was more crime. When he got a wife he would protect her and then she would owe him a great deal. Against all that was sacred he would prevail on her, he might be forced to tie her up in red underwear and attach a yoke to her. Bean was vigilant about his home and his guns were loaded. He regarded trespass as a dire offense and studied the tire marks and footprints neighbor and stranger made on the verge of his lawn. Bean's dog was as hair-triggered as he was, ruffing and flinching around the house like a creature beset by trespass at all stations. Both of them protected Bean's mother to distraction. She hauled him to and fro to doctors for his skin and in the waiting room thin Bean would rise to oppose whoever might cross his mother. Of all the boys, Bean most loved Swanly.

Three boys, Bean among them, waded out into a gravel pool now, a pool that moved heavy in its circumference but was still and deep in its center like a woman in the

very act of conception. The water moved past them into a
deep pit of sand under the bridge and then under the bluffs
on either side, terra-cotta besieged by black roots. An age-
less hermit bothersome to no one lived in some kind of tin
house in the bank down the way a half mile and they intended
to worry him. It was their fourth trip to the Strong and something was urgent now as they had to make plans. They were
not at peace and were hungry for an act before the age of
school job money and wife. The bittersweet Swanly named
it school job money whore, and felt ahead of him the awful
tenure in which a man shuffles up and down the lanes of a
great morgue. Swanly's father was a failure except for Swanly
himself who was beautiful past the genes of either parent.
He worshiped Swanly, idolized him, and heeded him, all he
said. He watched the smooth lad live life in his walk, talk,
and long silent tours in the bathtub. He believed in Swanly
as he did not himself or in his wife. It was Swanly's impression there was no real such thing as maturity, no, people
simply began acting like grown-ups, the world a farce of
playing house. Swanly of all the others most wanted an act,
standing there to his waist in the black water.

 The storekeeper Tuck knew for twenty years about
the clothesline strung from the shed at the rear of the yard
of the house behind the store. The T-bar stood at the near
end with high clover at its base. Yet that night two weeks
ago. His throat still hurt and had a red welt across it. He ran
through his lawn and necked himself on the wire. Blind in
the dark in a fury. What was it? All right. He had given himself up to age but although he did not like her he thought
his wife would hold out against it. After all she was ten years
younger. But he saw she was growing old in the shoulders
and under the eyes, all of a sudden. That might cause pity,
but like the awful old she had begun clutching things, hav-

ing her things, this time a box of Red Hots she wouldn't share, clutching it to her titties, this owning things more and more, small things and big, when he saw that he took a run across the yard, hard on baked mud, apoplectic, and the wire brought him down, a cutlass out of the dark. Now he was both angry and puny, riven and welted and all kind of ointment sticky at his shirt collar. It was intolerable especially now he'd seen the youth, oh wrath of loss, fair gone sprite. His very voice was bruised, the wound deep to the thorax.

Swanly, out in the river in old red shorts, was not a spoiled child. His father intended to spoil him but Swanly would not accept special privileges. He did not prevail by his looks or by his pocket money, a lot at hand always compared with the money of his partners, and he was not soft in any way so far that they knew. He could work, had worked, and he gave himself chores. He went to church occasionally, sitting down and eyed blissfully by many girls, many much older than Swanly. Even to his sluttish pill-addicted mother he was kind, even when she had some pharmaceutical cousin over on the occasion of his father being on the road. He even let himself be used as an adornment of her, with his mild temper and sad charm. She would say he would at any moment be kidnapped by Hollywood. And always he would disappear conveniently to her and the cousin as if he had never been there at all except as the ghost in the picture she kept.

Walthall with his German Mauser was naked in the pool. He had more hair than the others and on his chin the outline of a goatee. On his head was a dusty black beret and his eyes were set downriver at a broad and friendly horizon. But he would go in the navy. There was no money for college right away. His impressions were quicker and deeper than those of the others. By the time he knew something, it was in his roots as a passion. He led all aspirants in passion for music, weapons, girls, books, drinking, and wrestling, where operatic goons in mode just short of drag queens grappled in the city auditorium. Walthall, an actor, felt the act near too. He was a connoisseur and this act would be most delicious. He called the hermit's name.

Sunballs! Sunballs! hefting the Mauser, Lester Silk just behind him a foot shorter and like a wet rat with his big nose. Swanly stood in patient beatitude but with an itch on, Arden Pal and Bean away at the bluff. You been wantin' it, Sunballs! Been beggin' for it, called Silk.

Come get some! cried Bean, at that distance to Walthall a threatening hood ornament.

None could be heard very far in the noise of the river.

Tuck, who had followed in his car, did hear them from the bridge.

What could they want with that wretch Sunballs? he imagined.

He was not without envy of the hermit. What a mighty wound to the balls it must take to be like that, that hiding shuffling thing, harmless and beholden to no man. Without woman, without friend, without the asking of lucre, without all but butt-bare necessity. Haunt of the possum, coon, and crane, down there. Old Testament specters with birds all over them eating honey out of roadkill. Too good for men. Sunballs was not that old, either. But he was suddenly angry at the man. Above the fray, absent, out, was he? Well.

Tuck knelt beneath a cluster of poison sumac on the rim of the bluff. He saw the three naked in the water. There was Swanly in the pool, the blond hair, the tanned skin. Who dared give a south Mississippi pissant youth such powerful flow and comeliness? Already Tuck in his long depressed thinking knew the boy had no good father, his home would stink of distress. He had known his type in the Scouts, always something deep-warped at home with them, beauty thrown up out of manure like. The mother might be beautiful but this lad had gone early and now she was a tramp needed worship by any old bunch of rags around a pecker. A boy like that you had to take it slow but not that much was needed to replace the pa, in his dim criminal weakness. You had to show them strength then wait until possibly that day, that hour, that hazy fog of moment when thought required act, the kind hand of Tuck in an instant of transfer to all nexus below the navel, no more to be denied than those rapids they're hollering down, nice lips on the boy too.

You had to show them something, then be patient.

They hated Sunballs? I could thrash Sunballs. I can bury him, he thought. I am their man.

Tuck was angered against the hermit now but sickened too. The line of pain over his thorax he attributed now directly to the hermit. The hermit was confusion.

I am a vampire I am a vampire, Tuck said aloud. They shook me out of my nest and I can't be responsible for what might happen.

He knew the boy would be back at his store.

The storekeeper's sons were grown and fattish and ugly. They married and didn't even leave the community, were just up the road there nearly together. They both of them loved life and the parts hereabouts and he could not forgive them for it.

The boy would know something was waiting for him. It would take time but the something was nearly here. There had been warmth in their exchange, not all yet unpromising.

That night in another heat his wife spoke back to him. You ain't wanted it like this in a long time. What's come

over you. Now you be kindly be gentle you care for what
you want, silly fool.

As he spent himself he thought, Once after Korea
there was a chance for me. I had some fine stories about
Pusan, Inchon, and Seoul, not all of them lies. That I once
vomited on a gook in person. Fear of my own prisoner in
the frozen open field there, not contempt as I did explain.
But still. There was some money, higher education maybe,
big house in downtown Hawaii. But I had to put it all down
that hole, he said pulling back from the heat of his spouse.
The fever comes on you, you gasp like a man run out of the
sea by stingrays. Fore you know it you got her spread around
you like a tree and fat kids. You married a tree with a nest in
it blown and rained on every which way. You a part of the
tree too with your arms out legs out roots down ain't going
nowhere really even in an automobile on some rare break to
Florida, no you just a rolling tree.

But you get some scot-free thief of time like Sunballs,
he thinks he don't have to pay the toll. You know somebody
else somewhere is paying it for him, though. This person
rooted in his tree sweats the toll for Sunballs never you doubt
it. That wretch with that joker's name eases in the store
wanting to know whether he's paying sales tax, why is this
bit of bait up two cents from last time? Like maybe I ought
to take care of it for him. Like he's a double agent don't
belong to no country. Times twenty million you got the welfare army, biggest thing ever invaded this USA, say gimme
the money, the ham, the cheese, the car, the moon, worse
than Sherman's march. The babysitting, the hospital, throw
in a smoking Buick, and bad on gas mileage if you please.
Thanks very much kiss my ass. Army leech out this country
white and clay-dry like those bluffs over that river down
there. Pass a man with an honest store and friendly like

me, what you see is a man sucked dry, the suckee toting dat barge. The suckers drive by thirteen to the Buick like a sponge laughing at you with all its mouths, got that music too, mouths big from sucking the national tit sing it out like some banshee rat speared in the jungle.

Tuck had got himself in a sleepy wrath but was too tired to carry it out and would require a good short sleep, never any long ones anymore, like your old self don't want to miss any daylight, to lift himself and resume. That Swanly they called him, so fresh he couldn't even handle a Pall Mall.

There he was, the boy back alone like Tuck knew he would be. Something had happened between them. No wonder you kept climbing out of bed with this thing in the world this happy thing all might have come to.

It ain't pondering or chatting or wishing it's only the act, from dog to man to star all nature either exploding or getting ready to.

Tuck had seen a lot of him in the pool, the move of him. This one would not play sports. There was a lean sun-browned languor to him more apt for man than boy games. It went on beyond what some thick coach could put to use.

A sacred trust prevailing from their luck together would drive them beyond all judgment, man and adolescent boy against every ugly thing in that world, which would mean nothing anymore. He would look at fresh prospects again the same as when he the young warrior returned to these shores in '53. It would not matter how leeched and discommoded he had been for three decades. Put aside, step to joy.

You boys getting on all right sleeping over there? Tuck asked Swanly.

Where'd you hear we slept anywhere? The boy seemed in a trance between the aisles, the cans around him assorted junk of lowly needs. His hair was out of place from river, wind, and sand. Smears of bracken were on his pants knees, endearing him almost too much to Tuck. My dead little boyhood, Tuck almost sobbed.

I mean is nature being kind to you.

The boy half looked at him, panting a bit, solemn and bothered.

Are you in the drama club, young man?

Swanly sighed.

You sell acting lessons here at the store?

Good. Very quick. Somebody like you would be.

You don't know me at all.

Fourth year you've been at the river. I've sort of watched you grow at the store here, in a way. This time just a little sad, or mad. We got troubles?

We. Swanly peeked straight at him then quickly away.

When I was a little guy, Tuck spoke in his mind, I held two marbles in my hand just the blue-green like his eyes. It was across the road under those chinaberries and us tykes had packed the clay down in a near perfect circle. Shot all day looking at those pretty agates. Too good to play with. My fist was all sweaty around them. I'd almost driven them through my palm. The beauty of the balls. There inside my flesh. Such things drive you to a church you never heard of before, worship them.

I have no troubles, the boy said. No we either. No troubles.

You came back to the real world.

I thought I was in it.

You've come back all alone.

Outside there's a sign that says store, mister.

Down at the river pirates playhouse, you all.

Where you get your reality anyway? said the boy. Gas oil tobacco bacon hooks?

You know, wives can really be the gate of hell. They got that stare. They want to lock you down, get some partner to stoop down to that tiny peephole look at all the little shit with them. If you can forgive my language, ladies.

So you would be standing there 'mongst the Chesterfields seeing all the big?

Tuck did not take this badly. He liked the wit.

I might be. Some of us see the big things behind all the puny.

The hermit Sunballs appeared within the moment, the screen door slamming behind him like a shot. He walked on filthy gym shoes of one aspect with the soil of his wanderings, ripped up like the roots of it. You would not see such annealed textures at the ankles of a farmer, not this color of city gutters back long past. All of him the color of putty almost, as your eyes rose. The clothes vaporish like bus exhaust. The fingers whiter in the air like a potter's but he had no work and you knew this instantly. He held a red net sack for oranges, empty. It was not known why he had an interesting name like Sunballs. You would guess the one who had named him was the cleverer. Nothing in him vouched for parts solar. More perhaps of a star gray and dead or old bait or of a sex organ on the drowned. Hair thicket of red rust on gray atop him.

He poured over the tin tops in the manner of a devout scholar. The boy watched him in fury. It was the final waste product of all maturity he saw, a creature fired-out full molded by the world, the completed grown-up.

Whereas with an equal fury the storekeeper saw the man as the final insult to duty, friendless, wifeless, jobless, motherless, stateless, and not even black. He could not bear the nervous hands of the creature over his goods, arrogant discriminating moocher. He loathed the man so much a pain came in his head and his heartbeat had thrown a sweat on him. The presence of the boy broke open all gates and he loathed in particular with a hatred he had seldom known, certainly never in Korea, where people wearing gym shoes and smelling of garlic shot at him. Another mouth, Tuck thought, seeking picking choosing. He don't benefit nobody's day. Squandered every chance of his white skin, down in his river hole. Mocks even a healthy muskrat in personal hygiene. Not native to nothing. Hordes of them, Tuck imagined, pouring across the borders of the realm from bumland. His progeny lice with high attitudes.

Tuck saw the revulsion of the boy.

You ten cents higher than the store in Pinola, spoke Sunballs. His voice was shallow and thin as if he had worn it down screaming. A wreckage of teeth added a whistle at the end.

Tuck was invested by red blindness.

But Swanly spoke first. I warn you. Don't come near me. I can't be responsible, you.

The hermit whispered a breeze off rags where feral beings had swarmed. Ere be a kind of storeman take his neighbor by the short hairs like they got you dead in an airport and charges for water next thing you know.

What did you say? demanded the storekeeper coming around the register. You say neighbor and airport? You never even crossed through an airport I bet, you filthy mouthbroom.

Sunballs stood back from the beauty of Swanly but was not afraid of the anger of Tuck. He was too taken with this startling pretty boy.

Oh yes, my man, airport I have been in and the airplane crash is why I am here.

He pointed at the oiled floor swept clean by the wife who was now coming in from the rear in attendance to the loud voices, so rare in this shop, where the savage quiet reigned almost perpetual both sides of the mutual gloom, the weary armistice, then the hate and lust and panting. Only lately had her own beauty ebbed and not truly very much. She was younger with long muscular legs and dressed like a well-kept city woman in beach shorts. Her hair was brunette and chopped shortish and she had the skin of a Mexican. Her lips were pulled together in a purse someone might mistake for delight by their expression, not petulance. Her name was Bernadette and when Tuck saw her he flamed with nostalgia, not love. Brought back to his own hard tanned youth returned from the Orient on a ship in San Diego. Swanly looked over to her, and the two of them, boy and married woman, in the presence of the gasping hermit, fell in love.

What's wrong out here? she asked gently, her eyes never off the boy.

Said they can have it if that's what's there in the modern world, continued Sunballs. It was a good job I had too, I'm no liar. They was treating me special flying me to Kalamazoo, Michigan, on a Constellation. We was set upon by them flight stewards, grown men in matching suits, but they was these beatniks underneath, worse, these flight stewards, called, they attended themselves, it didn't matter men women or children, they was all homos all the time looking in a mirror at each other, didn't stir none atall for nobody else in their abomination once the airplane began crashing. It took forever rolling back and forth downward near like a corkscrew but we known it was plowing into ground directly. These two funny fellows you know, why when we wrecked all up with several dead up front and screaming, why they was in the back in the rear hull a'humpin' each other their eyes closed 'blivious to the crash they trying to get one last 'bomination in and we unlatched ourselves, stood up in the hulk and they still goin' at it, there's your modern world I say, two smoky old queers availing theyselve and the captain come back with half a burnt face say what the hell we got. Ever damn thing about it a crime against nature. No money no Kalamazoo never bring me back in, damn them, yes I seen it what it come down to in your modern world.

Tuck watched Swanly and his wife in long locked estimation of each other, the words of the hermit flying over like faraway geese.

People is going over to the other side of everything, I say, and it all roots out from the evil of price, the cost of everything being so goddamned high. Nothing ain't a tenth its value and a man's soul knows it's true.

What? Tuck said, down from his rage and confused by everybody. You ain't flapped on like this in the seven years you been prowling round.

Sunballs would not stop. Old man Bunch Lewis up north in the state, he run a store and has a hunchback. The hermit spoke with relish, struck loquacious by the act of love proceeding almost visibly between the boy and the wife, each to each, the female lips moving without words. It behooved him, he thought, to announce himself a wry soldier of the world.

Fellow come in seen Lewis behind the counter with a ten-dollar shirt in his hands. Said Lewis, What's that on your back? Lewis got all fierce, he say, You know it's a hump I'm a humpback you son of a bitch. Fellow say, Well I thought it might be your ass, everything else in this store so high. What he say.

Neither the storekeeper nor his wife had ever heard the first word of wit from this man.

The hermit put a hand to his rushy wad of hair as if to groom it. The plain common man even in this humble state can't afford no clothes where you got the Bunch Lewises a'preying on them, see. After this appeal he paused, shot out for a time, years perhaps.

This isn't a plain common boy here, though, is he, son? Bernadette said, as if her voice had fled out and she powerless. The question called out of her in a faint tone between mother love and bald lechery. Is it real? Has this boy escaped out of a theater somewheres? demanded the hermit. His eyes were on the legs of the wife, her feet set in fashion huaraches like a jazz siren between the great wars.

You never even looked at my wife before, said Tuck. Pissmouth.

Hush everybody. You getting the air dirty, said Bernadette.

Her own boys were hammy and homely and she wandered in a moment of conception, giving birth to Swanly all over again as he stood there, a pained ecstasy in the walls of her womb. He was what she had intended by everything female about her and she knew hardly any woman ever chanced to see such a glorious boy.

Tuck was looking at her afresh and he was shocked. Why my wife, she's a right holy wonder, she is, he thought. Or is she just somebody I've not ever seen now?

Out of the south Mississippi fifth-grown pines, the rabbitweed, the smaller oaks and hickories, the white clay and the coon-toed bracken, she felt away on palisades over a sea of sweetening terror.

She said something nobody caught. Swanly in shyness and because he could not hold his feelings edged away with a can of sardines and bottle of milk unpaid for, but he was not conscious of this.

I am redeemed, she said again, even more softly.

Sunballs left with a few goods unpaid for and he was very conscious of this. Tuck stared at him directly as he went out the door but saw little. It must have been the hermit felt something was owed for his narration.

The wife walked to the screen and looked out carefully.

You stay away from that boy, she called, and they heard her.

When Tuck was alone behind the register again he sensed himself alien to all around him and his aisles seemed a fantastic dump of road offal brought in by a stranger.

He was in the cold retreat from Chosin marching backwards, gooks in the hills who'd packed in artillery by donkey. You could smell the garlic coming off them at a half mile but My sweet cock that was my living room compared to this now, he thought.

All the fat on him, the small bags under his eyes, the hint of rung at his belt he summoned out of himself. He must renew his person. Some moments would come and he could do this simply by want. Tuck felt himself grow leaner and handsomer.

Walthall had wanted the peach wine to become brandy but alas. He brought his viola to the river camp and Pal his bass flute, two instruments unrecognized by anybody in his school, his city, and they played them passing strange with less artistry than vengeance sitting opposed on a sunken petrified log like an immense crocodile forced up by saurian times, in the first rush of small rapids out of the pool. This river in this place transported them to Germany or the Rockies or New England, anywhere but here, and the other boys, especially the hearkening beatific Swanly, listened, confident paralyzed hipsters, to the alien strains of these two mates, set there in great parlor anguish swooning like people in berets near death.

Bean, the sternest and most religious of them all, set his gun on his knees, feeling a lyric militancy and praying for an enemy. Like the others, this boy was no drinking man but unlike them he did not drink the wine from the fruit jars. For the others, the wine went down like a ruined orchard, acid to the heart, where a ball of furred heat made them reminiscent of serious acts never acted, women never had.

The wine began dominating and the boys were willing slaves. When the music paused Lester Silk, son of the decaying army man who never made anything but fun of poetry and grabbed his scrotum and acted the fairy whenever it occurred at school, said, I believe in years to come I will meet a pale woman from Texas who plays clarinet in the symphony. Then we shall dally, there will be a rupture over my drinking, she'll tear up my pictures and for penance over the freedoms she allowed me she will go off to the nun mountains in a faraway state and be killed accidentally by masked gunmen. Forever afterward I will whup my lap mournfully in her memory.

Somebody must die when you hear that music out here, I feel it, said Swanly, cool-butted and naked in the little rapids but full hot with the peach wine after five swallows.

Walthall, stopping the viola, wore a necklace of twine and long mail-order Mauser shells. He exclaimed, Send not to ask for when the bell tolls. I refuse to mourn the death by fire of a child's Christmas on Fern Hill. Do not go gently in my sullen craft, up yours. He raised the fruit jar from his rock.

All that separates me from Leslie Caron must die, said Arden Pal. He held his flute up like a saber, baroque over the flat rocks and frothing tea of the rapids. Pal was a gangling youth of superfluous IQ already experiencing vile depressions. His brain made him feel constantly wicked but he relieved himself through botany and manic dilettantism.

Like a piece of languid Attic statuary Swanly lay out with a sudden whole nudeness under the shallow water. He might have been something caught in the forest and detained for study, like a white deer missing its ilk, because he was sad and in love and greatly confused.

Bernadette cooked two chickens, made a salad, then Irish Creme cookies, for the boys' health, she said, for their wretched motherless pirates' diets, and Tuck drove her down to the bridge with it all in a basket. Catastrophic on both sides of the washboard gravel was the erosion where ditches of white limesoil had been clawed into deep small canyons by heavy rains, then swerved into the bogs in wild fingers. Tuck pretended he was confused as to where the boys might be in camp and guessed loudly while pulling off before the bridge into the same place he had been earlier. Ah, he said, the back of their car, Hinds County, I recognize it.

But he said he would wait and that was perfect by Bernadette. Then he followed her, tree to tree, at a distance. Bernadette came to the head of the bluff and he saw her pause, then freeze, cradling the food basket covered in blue cloth with white flowers printed on. Through a nearer gully he saw what she saw.

Hairy Walthall, at the viola with his root floating in the rills, might have seemed father to Swanly, who was hung out like a beige flag in the shallows. She could not see Arden Pal but she heard the deep weird flute. Swanly moved as a liquid one with the river, the bed around him slick tobacco shale, and Bernadette saw all this through a haze of inept but solemn chamber music. She did not know it was inept and a wave of terrible exhilaration overcame her.

Tuck looked on at the boys from his own vantage, stroking the wound to his throat.

The hermit Sunballs was across the river before them in a bower of wild muscadine, prostrate and gripping the lip of the bluff. He owned a telescope, which he was now using. He viewed all of Swanly he could. The others were of no concern. For a while Tuck and his wife could not see him, flat to the earth and the color of organic decay. None of them for that matter would have recognized their own forms rapt and helpless to the quick, each with their soul drawn out through their eyes, beside themselves, stricken into painful silence.

It was habitual with Pal as he played the flute, however, that his eyes went everywhere. He was unsure at first then he thought he had invoked ghosts by his music, the ancient river dead roused from their Civil War ghoulments by the first flute since in these parts. He was startled by this for the seconds the thought lasted then he was frightened because they were on both bluffs and he mistook the telescope pushed out of the vines for a weapon. Perhaps they were the law, but next he knew they were not, seeing one was a woman.

They're watching you, Swanly!

The boys, except Swanly, came out of the water and thrashed back to the camp incensed and indignant. Pal pointed his flute at the telescope, which receded. Then the hermit's face came briefly into the frame of vine leaves. He could not tear himself away.

Swanly stood wobbling in the shallows, his hand to the slick shale rock, then at last stood up revealed and fierce in his nakedness. He swayed on the slick rocks, outraged, screaming. Then he vomited.

Keep your eyes off me! Keep away! he bawled upwards at the hermit, who then disappeared.

Pal pointed upwards to the right. They watched too, Swanly! But Swanly didn't seem to understand this.

Walthall fired his Mauser twice in the air and the blasts made rocking echoes down the river beach to beach.

Bernadette and Tuck melted back onto the rooted path in the high cane and the woman came cautiously with her basket, trailed fifty yards behind by her husband who was trembling and homicidal toward the hermit. Also he knew the boy loved his wife more than him. The boy's nakedness to him had had no definition but was a long beige flag of taunting and every fine feeling of his seemed mocked and whored by the presence of the hermit. Tuck felt himself only a raving appendage to the event, a thing tacked on to the crisis of his wife.

Yoo hoo! Oh bad bad boys. I've got a treat for you, called Bernadette. All wet in their pants they stared up to the woman clearing the cane above them, their beds spread below her. Their sanctuary ruined. Only Swanly knew who she was.

Oh no, is it a woman of the church? said Walthall.

There will always be a woman around to wreck things, said Pal.

No, she's all right, Swanly intervened, though he was still sick. He came up from the shore roots and struggled into his shorts slowly. He seemed paralyzed and somewhere not with them, an odd sleepiness on him. Be nice, all of you, he added.

Big Mama Busybod, said Walthall. Courtesy of the Southern regions.

Out in the sun they saw she was not a bad-looking case though she seemed arrested by a spiritual idea and did not care her hair was blowing everywhere like a proper woman of the '50s would.

Her husband came behind, mincing over the stone beach. She turned.

I heard the shots, he said.

Fools. Eat, said Bernadette. But she remained startled by Swanly and could not turn her face long from him.

Tuck didn't understand it, but his jaw began flapping. You boys ever bait a trotline with soap? Yes Ivory soap. Tuck pointed under the bridge where their line was set on the near willow. Tuck was not convinced he even existed now outside the river of want he poured toward Swanly. He was not interested in what he continued to say, like something in a storekeeper's costume activated by a pullstring and thrust into a playhouse by a child. Fish began biting on the substances of modern industry in the '40s, boys. Why they're like contemporary men they ain't even that hungry just more curious. Or a woman. They get curious and then the bait eats them, huh.

Yes sir, said Walthall, annoyed.

Tuck kept on in despondent sagery then trailed off as the boys ate and he next simply sat down on a beach boulder and stared away from them into the late bower of Sunballs across the river.

When he twisted to look he was astounded by the extent of bosom his wife was visiting on Swanly. She was bared like some tropical hula but not. Swanly ate his chicken kneeling in front of her with his bare smooth chest slightly burned red and of such an agreeable shape he seemed made to fly through night winds like the avatar on the bow of a ship. That hussy had dropped her shawl down and Tuck noticed more of her in truth, her mothersome cleavage, than he had in years, faintly freckled and still not a bad revelation. Not in years atop her.

It was eleven years ago when he had pursued illicit love with another woman. This was when his boys were small and cute. He could not get over how happy he was and blameless and blessed-feeling, as if in the garden before the fall. She was a young woman with practical headquarters in the Jackson Country Club, a thing he felt giant pride about, her sitting there in a swimsuit nursing a Tom Collins, high-heeled beach shoes on her feet, talking about storms how she loved them. Now she was a fat woman and his children were fat men and it was not their fatness that depressed him so much as it was watching visible time on them, the horrible millions of minutes collected and evident, the murdered idle thousands of hours, his time more than theirs in their change. They had an unfortunate disease where you saw everything the minute you saw them, the awful feckless waiting, the lack of promise, the bulk of despair. The woman had been attracted to him through his handsome little boys and she would excite him by exclaiming, Oh what wonderful seed you have. He stayed up like a happy lighthouse with rotating beam. She had no children, never would, but she whispered to him he might break her will if he didn't stop being so good. All the while he had loved Bernadette too, even more, was that possible? The woman didn't mind. What kind of man am I? Tuck thought. Was time working every perversion it had on him, were there many like him? He felt multiplied in arms and legs, a spider feeling eight ways, he was going into the insect kingdom. Oh yes, lost to the rest.

He loved his boys but my God they were like old uncles, older than him, mellow and knee-slapping around a campfire. He loved his wife, but no he didn't, it was an embattled apathy each morning goaded into mere courtesy, that was what, and he felt wild as a prophet mocking an army of the righteous below him at the gate.

Now isn't that better? his wife said to the boys, who had fed themselves with hesitation before they fell to trough like swine.

You're too thoughtful of us, ma'am, said Swanly.

I'm Bernadette, she said.

You are desperate, thought Tuck. I sort of like it. Hanging all out there, little Mama.

Was it how you like it? she said only to the boy.

My mother never cooked for me like that.

Ah.

Nobody ever has.

Oh. What's wrong?

That hermit, you know. He saw me without anything on.

She could see he was still trembling, warm as it was.

I know how it is. She looked more deeply into his eyes. Believe me.

What is it? said Tuck, coming up.

This boy's been spied on by that creature Sunballs.

Tuck leaned in to Swanly. The boy was evilly shaken like a maiden thing out of the last century. He was all boy but between genders, hurt deep to his modesty. Tuck was greatly curious and fluttered-up. All execrable minutes, all time regained. I would live backwards in time until I took the shape of the boy myself. My own boyself was eat up by the gooks and then this strolling wench, my boyself was hostaged by her, sucking him out to her right in front of me, all over again as with me. Woman's thing stays hungry, it don't diminish, it's always something. A need machine, old

beard lost its teeth harping on like a holy fool in the desert.
They're always with themselves having sex with themselves,
two lips forever kissing each other down there and they got
no other subject. Even so, I feel love for her all over again.

Lester Silk, Bean, and Pal studied this trio isolated
there where the water on rills avid over pebbles made a laughing noise. Walthall raised his viola and spread his arms out
like a crucified musician and he stood there in silence evok-
ing God knows what but Arden Pal asked the others what
was going on.

Wake up and smell the clue, whispered Silk. Walthall
wants the woman and our strange boy Swanly's already
got her.

Swanly's okay, Silk. He's not strange.

Maybe not till now.

Leave him alone, said Bean. Swanly's a right guy.
He has been through some things that's all. Ask me.

You mean a dead daddy like you?

I'd say you look hard enough, a dead both, but he
wouldn't admit it. Bean intended to loom there in his acu-
ity for a moment, looking into the breech of his gun which
he had opened with the lever. It was a rare lever action shotgun, 20-gauge. Bean worshiped shells and bullets. Ask me,
he's a full orphan.

They blending with him, said Arden Pal. They
watched us naked too. She didn't jump back in the bushes
like a standard woman when I caught her.

Swanly came over getting his shirt.

She's giving me something. I'm feeling poorly,
he said.

The rest did not speak and the three, Tuck, Bernadette, and Swanly, walked up the shallow bluff and into
the woods.

Silk sighed. I don't quite believe I ever seen nothing like that. Old store boy there looks like somebody up to the eight count.

Walthall, who had actually had a sort of girl, since with stubborn farm boy will he would penetrate nearly anything sentient, was defeated viola and all. Lord my right one for mature love like that. No more did he heed the calling of his music and he was sore in gloom.

Bean could not sit still and he walked here and there rolling two double-aught buckshot shells in his palm, looking upward to the spying bower of the hermit, but no offending eye there now, as he would love.

They closed the store as Swanly began talking. She went to the house and got something for his belly and some nerve pills too and diet pills as well. Bernadette was fond of both diet and nerve pills, and sometimes her husband was too, quite positively. Some mornings they were the only promise he could fetch in and he protected his thefts of single pills from his wife's cabinet with grim slyness. In narcosis she was fond of him and in amphetamine zeal he returned affection to her which she mistook for actual interest. The doctor in Magee was a firm believer in Dexamil as panacea and gave her anything she wanted. The pain of wanting in her foreign eyes got next to him. In a fog of charity he saw her as a lovely spy in the alien pines. He saw a lot of women and few men who weren't in the act of bleeding as they spoke, where they stood. The pharmacist was more a partisan of Demerol and John Birch and his prices were high since arsenals were expensive. His constant letters to Senator McCarthy, in his decline, almost consumed his other passions for living, such as they were. But the pharmacist liked Bernadette too, and when she left, detained as long as he could prolong the difficulty of her prescription, he went in the back room where a mechanic's calendar with a picture of a woman lying cross-legged in a dropped halter on the hood of a Buick was nailed to the wall and laid hand to himself. One night the doctor and the pharmacist met in this room and began howling like wolves in lonely ardor. Bernadette's name was mentioned many times, then they would howl again. They wore female underwear but were not sodomites. Both enjoyed urban connections and their pity for Bernadette in her aging beauty out in the river boonies was painful without limit; and thus in the proper lingerie they acted it out.

Swanly, after the pills, began admitting to the peach wine as if it were a mortal offense. Bernadette caught his spirit. They adjourned to the house where he could lie comfortably with her Oriental shawl over him.

We don't have strong drink here. Not much. She looked to Tuck. You don't have to drink to have a full experience.

Tuck said, No, not drink. Hardly.

No. I'm having fun just talking. Talking to you is fine. Because I haven't been much of a talker. That's good medicine. My tongue feels all light.

Talk on, child. She gave Swanly another pill.

Tuck went to relieve himself and through the window he saw the clothesline over the green clover and he speculated that through time simple household things might turn on you in a riot of overwhelming redundancy. He had heard of a man whose long dear companion, a buckskin cat, had walked between his legs one night and tripped and killed him as he went down headfirst onto a commode. Cheered that this was not him he went back to listen to the boy.

But after all you wouldn't have just anybody look at you all bared. Surely not that awful person, Bernadette was saying. I'd not let him see me for heaven's sake.

It seems he ought to pay. I feel tortured and all muddy. I can't forget it.

Just talk it out, that's best. It seems there's always a monster about, doesn't it?

I feel I could talk all afternoon into the night.

We aren't going anywhere.

We aren't going anywhere, added Tuck.

I'm feeling all close to you if that's all right.

Some people are sent to us. We have been waiting all our lives for somebody and don't even know it.

Older ones are here to teach and guide the young, Tuck said.

Bernadette glanced at Tuck then looked again. He had come back with his hair combed and he had shaved. He was so soft in the face she felt something new for him. In this trinity already a pact was sealed and they could no more be like others. There was a tingling and a higher light around them. A flood of goodwill took her as if they had been hurled upon a foreign shore, all fresh. The boy savior, child, and paramour at once. Swanly spoke on, it hardly mattered what he said. Each word a pleasant weight on her bosom.

Walthall and the rest stared into the fire sighing, three of them having their separate weather, their separate fundament, in peach wine. Pal could swallow no more and heaved out an arc of puke luminous over the fire, crying, Thar she blows, my dear youth. This act was witnessed like a miracle by the others.

God in heaven, this stuff was so good for a while, said Silk.

Fools, said Bean.

Bean don't drink because he daddy daid, said Walthall. So sad, so sad, so gone, so Beat.

Yeh. It might make him cry, said Pal.

Or act human, said Silk.

Let it alone. Bean had stood unmoved by their inebriation for two hours, caressing his 20-gauge horse gun.

Teenage love, teenage heart. My face broke out the other night but I'm in love wit yewwww! sang Walthall.

What you think Swanly's doing, asked Pal.

Teenage suckface. Dark night of the suck.

They are carrying him away, far far away, Silk declared.

Or him them.

Having a bit of transversion, them old boy and girl.

You mean travesty. Something stinketh, I tell you.

We know.

The hermit made Swanly all sick. We should put a stop to his mischief, said Bean all sober.

That person saw the peepee full out of ourn good friend ourn little buddy.

This isn't to laugh about. Swanly's deep and he's a hurting man.

Boy, said Pal. He once told me every adult had a helpless urge to smother the young so they could keep company with the dead, which were themselves.

You'd have to love seeing small animals suffer to hurt Swanly. The boy's damn near an angel. I swear he ain't even rightly one of us, said Silk. Bean did not care for Silk, who had only joined them lately. But Silk redeemed himself, saying, Christ I'm just murky. Swanly's deep.

You know what, Walthall spoke, I felt sorry for all three of them when they left here. Yes the woman is aged but fine, but it was like a six-legged crippled thing.

So it was, said Pal. I declare nothing happy is going on wherever they are.

★ ★ ★

Whosoever you are, be that person with all your might. Time goes by faster than we thought. It is a thief so quiet. You must let yourself be loved and you must love, parts of you that never loved must open and love. You must announce yourself in all particulars so you can have yourself.

Tuck going on at dawn. Bernadette was surprised again by him. Another man, fluent, had risen in his place. She was in her pink sleeping gown but the others wore their day clothes and were not sleepy.

Listen, the birds are singing for us out there and it's a morning, a real morning, Bernadette said. A true morning out of all the rest of the mornings.

By noon they were hoarse and languid and commended themselves into a trance wherein all wore bedsheets and naked underneath they moved about the enormous bed like adepts in a rite. The question was asked of Swanly by Tuck whether he would care to examine their lovely Bernadette since he had never seen a woman and Swanly said yes and Bernadette lay back opening the sheet and then spreading herself so Swanly saw a woman as he had never seen her for a long while and she only a little shy and the boy smiled wearily assenting to her glory and was pulled inward through love and death and constant birth gleefully repeated by the universe. Then husband and wife embraced with the boy between them on the edge of the bed, none of them recalling how they were there but all talk ceased and they were as those ignorant animals amongst the fruit of Eden just hours before the thunder.

Long into the afternoon they awoke with no shame and only the shyness of new dogs in a palace and then an abashed hunger for the whole ritual again set like a graven image in all their dreams. The boy had been told things and he felt very elegant, a crowned orphan now orphan no more. Bernadette, touched in all places, felt dear and coveted. All meanness had been driven from Tuck and he was blank in an ecstasy of separate parts like a creature torn to bits at the edge of a sea. Around them were their scattered clothes, the confetti of delirium. They embraced and were suspended in a bulb of void delicate as a drop of water.

Sunballs came around the store since it was closed and he wore a large knife on his belt in a scabbard with fringe on it and boots in white leather and high to the knee, which he had without quite knowing their use rescued out of a country lane near the bridge, the jetsam of a large majorette seduced in a car he had been watching all night. At the feet he looked blindingly clean as in a lodge ceremony. He walked quickly as if appointed and late. He looked in one window of the blue house, holding the sill, before he came to the second and beheld them all naked gathering and ungathering in languor, unconscious in their innocence. He watched a goodly while, his hands formally at his side, bewitched like a pole-axed angel. Then he commenced rutting on the scabbard of his knife grabbed desperately to his loins but immediately also to call out scolding as somebody who had walked up on murder.

Cursed and stunned Tuck and Bernadette snatched the covering but Swanly sat peering at the fiend outside until overcome by grief and then nausea. His nudity was then like one dead, cut down from joy. Still, he was too handsome, and Sunballs could not quit his watching while Swanly retched himself sore.

He might well be dying, thought Sunballs, and this fascinated him, these last heavings of beauty. He began to shake and squalled even louder. There was such a clamor from the two adults he awoke to himself and hastened back to the road and into the eroded ditch unbraked until he

reached his burrow. Under his bluff the river fled deep and
black with a sheen of new tar, and the hermit emerged once
on his filthy terrace to stand over it in conversation with his
erection, his puny calves in the white boots.

The boys labored with oaths down the bedrocks of
the river. All was wretched and foul since waking under the
peach wine, which they now condemned, angry at daylight
itself. Only Bean was ready to the task. They went through
a bend in silence and approached water with no beach. They
paused for a while then flung in and waded cold to their
chests. Bean, the only one armed, carried the cavalry shotgun above his head.

I claim this land for the Queen of Spain, Bean said.
God for a hermit to shoot. My kingdom for a hermit. Then
he went underwater but the shotgun stayed up and dry,
waggled about.

When he came up he saw the hermit leering down
from his porch on the bluff. Bean, choked and bellicose,
thought he heard Sunballs laughing at him. He levered
in a round and without hesitation would have shot the
man out of his white boots had this person not been
snatched backwards by Tuck. All of them saw the arm come
around his neck and the female boots striding backwards in
air, then dust in vacant air, the top of a rust hut behind it. A
stuffed holler went off the bluff and scattered down the
pebble easements westerly and into the cypresses on either
side. Then there was silence.

He was grabbed by something, said Walthall, something just took Sunballs away.

By hell, I thought he was shot before I pulled the
trigger, swore Bean. Bean had horrified himself. The horse
gun in his hand was loathsome.

Don't hit me no more in the eye! a voice cried from
above.

Then there were shouts from both men and much stomping on the terrace.

Tuck shrieked out, his voice like a great bird driving past. They heard then the hysterical voice of Swanly baying like a woman. The boys were spooked but drawn. They went to finding a path upwards even through the wine sickness.

Swanly, he ain't right and that's him, said Pal.

Well somebody's either humping or killing somebody.

We charging up there like we know what to do about it.

I could've killed him, said Bean, dazed still. Damn you Swanly. For you, damn you.

Then they were up the fifty feet or more and lost in cane through which they heard groans and sobs. They turned to this and crashed through and to the man they were afraid. At the edge of the brake, they drew directly upon a bin buried three-quarters in the top of the bluff, this house once a duckblind. In front of it from the beaten clay porch they heard sounds and they pressed around to them like harried pilgrims anxious for bad tidings. They saw the river below open up in a wide bend deep and strong through a passage of reigning boulders on either side and then just beside them where they had almost overwalked them, Bernadette and Swanly together on the ground, Swanly across her lap and the woman with her breasts again nearly out of their yoke in a condition of the Pietà, but Swanly red and mad in the face, both of them covered with dust as if they had rolled through a desert together. This put more fear in them than would have a ghoul, and they looked quickly away where Tuck sat holding his slashed stomach, beside him the hermit spread with outstretched boots, swatted down as from some pagan cavalry. Sunballs covered his eyes with his hands.

They thought in those seconds that Tuck had done

himself in. The big hunting knife was still in his hand and he gazed over the river as if dying serenely. But this was only exhaustion and he looked up at them unsurprised and baleful as if nothing more could shock him.

I can't see, moaned Sunballs. He never stopped hitting my eyes.

Good, good, spoke Tuck. I'm not sorry. Cut your tongue out next, tie you up in a boat down that river. See how you spy on those sharks in the Gulf of Mexico.

I ain't the trouble, moaned the hermit. You got big sons wouldn't think so either.

Nothing stands between me and that tongue, keep wagging it.

Them ole boys of yours could sorely be enlightened.

Sunballs moved his hands and the boys viewed the eyes bruised like a swollen burglar's mask, the red grief of pounded meat in the sockets. The fingers of both Tuck's hands were mud red and fresher around the knife handle. But Tuck was spent, a mere chattering head, and the hermit in his agony rolled over and stared blind into his own vomit. His wadded hair was white-flecked by it and the boys didn't look any more at him.

It was Swanly they loved and could not bear to see. He was not the bright shadow of their childhoods anymore, he was not the boy of almost candescent complexion, he was not the pal haunting in the remove of his beauty, slim and clean in his limbs. This beauty had been a strange thing. It had always brought on some distress and then infinite kindness in others and then sadness too. But none of them were cherubs any longer and they knew all this and hated it, seeing him now across the woman's lap, her breasts over his twisted face. Eden in the bed of Eros, all Edenwide all lost. He was neither child, boy, nor man, and he was dreadful. Bean could barely carry on and knelt before him in idiocy. Walthall was enraged, big hairy Walthall, viola torn to bits inside him. He could not forgive he was ever obliged to see this.

We're taking our friend with us.

You old can have each other, said Bean. He had forgot the shotgun in his hand.

Bury each other. Take your time.

The woman looked up, her face flocked with dust.

We're not nasty. We were good people.

Sure. Hag.

Come on away, Bean, Pal directed him.

Bring Swanly up. Hold him, somebody, help me. Walthall was large and clumsy. He could not see the way to handle Swanly.

Bernadette began to lick the dust from Swanly's cheeks.

There ain't nothing only a tiny light, and a round dark, sighed Sunballs. It ain't none improved.

We are bad. Tuck spoke. Damn us, damn it all.

Silk and Pal raised Swanly up and although he was very sick he could walk. There was an expression simian wasted on his face, blind to those who took him now, blind to the shred of clothes remaining to him, his shorts low on his hips.

They kept along the gravel shoulder the mile back to their camp. Bean with the handsome gun, relic of swaggering days in someone else's life. He seemed deputized and angry, walking Swanly among the others. Sometimes Swanly fell from under him completely, his legs surrendered, while they pulled him on, no person speaking.

In the halls of his school thenceforward Swanly was wolfish in his glare and often dirty. In a year no one was talking to him at all. The exile seemed to make him smile but as if at others inside himself he knew better than them.

His mother, refractory until this change in her son, withdrew into silent lesbian despair with another of her spirit then next into a church and out of this world, where her husband continued to make his inardent struggles.

Some fourteen years later, big Walthall, rich but sad, took a sudden turn off the regular highway on the way to a Florida vacation. He was struck by a nostalgia he could not account for, like a bole of overweening sad energy between his eyes. He drove right up to the store and later he swore to Bean and Pal that although Tuck had died, an almost unrecognizable and clearly mad old woman hummed, nearly toothless, behind the cash register. She was wearing Swanly's old jersey, what was left of it, and the vision was so awful he fled almost immediately and was not right in Boca Raton nor much better when he came back home.

When Walthall inquired about the whereabouts of Swanly the woman began to scream without pause.

A Creature in the
Bay of St. Louis

WE WERE OUT EARLY IN THE BROWN WATER, THE LIGHT STILL gray and wet.

My cousin Woody and I were wading on an oyster shell reef in the bay. We had cheap bait-casting rods and reels with black cotton line at the end of which were a small bell weight and a croaker hook. We used peeled shrimp for bait. Sometimes you might get a speckled trout or flounder but more likely you would catch the croaker. A large one weighed a half pound. When caught and pulled in the fish made a metallic croaking sound. It is one of the rare fish who talk to you about their plight when they are landed. My aunt fried them crispy, covered in cornmeal, and they were delicious, especially with lemon juice and ketchup.

A good place to fish was near the pilings of the Saint Stanislaus school pier. The pier gate was locked but you could wade to the pilings and the oyster shell reef. Up the bluff above us on the town road was a fish market and the Star Theater, where we saw movies.

Many cats, soft and friendly and plump, would gather around the edges of the fish market and when you went to the movies you would walk past three or four of them who would ease against your leg as if asking to go to the movie with you. The cats were very social. In their prosperity they seemed to have organized into a watching society of leisure and culture. Nobody yelled at them because this was a very small coastal town where everybody knew each other. Italians, Slavs, French, Negroes, Methodists, Baptists, and Catholics. You did not want to insult the cat's owner by

rudeness. Some of the cats would tire of the market offer-
ings and come down the bluff to watch you fish, patiently
waiting for their share of your take or hunting the edges of
the weak surf for dead crabs and fish. You would be pulling
in your fish, catch it, and when you looked ashore the cats
were alert suddenly. They were wise. It took a hard case not
to leave them one good fish for supper.

That night as you went into an Abbott and Costello
movie, which cost a dime, that same cat you had fed might
rub against your leg and you felt sorry it couldn't go into
the movie house with you. You might be feeling comical
when you came out and saw the same cat waiting with conviction as if there were something in there it wanted very
much, and you threw a Jujube down to it on the sidewalk. A
Jujube was a pellet of chewing candy the quality of vulca-
nized rubber. You chewed several during the movie and you
had a wonderful syrup of licorice, strawberry, and lime in
your mouth. But the cat would look down at the Jujube then
up at you as if you were insane, and you felt badly for be-
traying this serious creature and hated that you were mean
and thoughtless. That is the kind of conscience you had in
Bay St. Louis, Mississippi, where you were always close to
folks and creatures.

This morning we had already had a good trip as the
sun began coming out. The croakers swam in a burlap sack
tied to a piling and underwater. The sacks were free at the
grocery and people called them croaker sacks. When you
lifted the sack to put another croaker in you heard that froggy
metal noise in a chorus, quite loud, and you saw the cats on
shore hearken to it too. We would have them with french-
fried potatoes, fat tomato slices from my uncle's garden, and
a large piece of deep sweet watermelon for supper.

It made a young boy feel good having the weight of all these fish in the dripping sack when you lifted it, knowing you had provided for a large family and maybe even neighbors at supper. You felt to be a small hero of some distinction, and ahead of you was that mile walk through the neighborhood lanes where adults would pay attention to your catch and salute you. The fishing rod on your shoulder, you had done some solid bartering with the sea, you were not to be trifled with.

The only dangerous thing in the bay was a stingaree, with its poisonous barbed hook of a tail. This ray would lie flat covered over by sand like a flounder. We waded barefoot in swimming trunks and almost always in a morning's fishing you stepped on something that moved under your foot and you felt the squirm in every inch of your body before it got off from you. These could be stingarees. There were terrible legends about them, always a story from summers ago when a stingaree had whipped its tail into the calf of some unfortunate girl or boy and buried the vile hook deep in the flesh. The child came dragging out of the water with this twenty-pound brownish-black monster the size of a garbage can lid attached to his leg, thrashing and sucking with its awful mouth. Then the child's leg grew black and swelled hugely and they had to amputate it, and that child was in the attic of some dark house on the edge of town, never the same again and pale like a thing that never saw light, then eventually the child turned into half-stingaree and they took it away to an institution for special cases. So you believed all this most positively and when a being squirmed under your foot you were likely to walk on water out of there. We should never forget that when frightened a child can fly short distances too.

The high tide was receding with the sun clear up and smoking in the east over Biloxi, the sky reddening, and the croakers were not biting so well anymore. But each new fish would give more pride to the sack and I was greedy for a few more since I didn't get to fish in salt water much. I lived four hours north in a big house with a clean lawn, a maid, and yardmen, but it was landlocked and grim when you compared it to this place of my cousin's. Much later I learned his family was nearly poor, but this was laughable even when I heard it, because it was heaven: the movie house right where you fished and the society of cats, and my uncle's house with the huge watermelons lying on the linoleum under the television with startling shows like "Lights Out!" from the New Orleans station. We didn't even have a television station yet where I lived.

I kept casting and wading out deeper toward an old creosoted pole in the water where I thought a much bigger croaker or even a flounder might be waiting. My cousin was tired and red-burnt from yesterday in the sun, so he went to swim under the diving board of the Catholic high school a hundred yards away. They had dredged a pool. Otherwise the sea was very shallow a long ways out. But now I was almost up to my chest, near the barnacled pole where a big boat could tie up. I kept casting and casting, almost praying toward the deep water around the pole for a big fish. The lead and shrimp would plunk and tumble into a dark hole, I thought, where a special giant fish was lurking, something too big for the croaker shallows.

My grandmother had caught a seven-pound flounder from the sea wall years ago and she was still honored for it, my uncle retelling the tale about her whooping out, afraid but happy, the pole bent double. I wanted to have a story like that about me. The fish made Mama Hannah so happy, my older cousin said, that he saw her dancing to a band on

television by herself when everybody else was asleep. Soon—
I couldn't bear to think about it—in a couple of days they
would drive me over to Gulfport and put me on a bus for
home, and in my sorrow there waited a dry red brick school
within bitter tasting distance. But even that would be sweet-
ened by a great fish and its story.

It took place in no more than half a minute, I'd
guess, but it had the lengthy rapture and terror of a whole
tale. Something bit and then was jerking, small but solidly,
then it was too big, and I began moving in the water and
grabbing the butt of the rod again because what was on had
taken it out of my hands. When I caught the rod up, I was
moving toward the barnacled pole with the tide slopping
on it, and that was the only noise around. I went in to my
neck in a muddier scoop in the bottom, and then under
my feet something moved. I knew it was a giant stingaree
instantly. Hard skin on a squirming plate of flesh. I was
sorely terrified but was pulled even past this and could do
nothing, now up to my chin and the stiff little pole bent
violently double. I was dragged through the mud and I
knew the being when it surfaced would be bigger than me
and with much more muscle. Then, like something underwater since Europe, seven or eight huge purpoises surfaced,
blowing water in a loud group explosion out of their enormous heads, and I was just shot all over with light and
nerves because they were only twenty feet from me and I
connected them, the ray, and what was on my hook into a
horrible combination beast that children who waded too
far would be dragged out by and crushed and drowned.

The thing pulled with heavier tugs like a truck going
up its gears. The water suddenly rushed into my face and
into my nose, I could see only brown with the bottom of the
sun shining through it.

I was gone, gone, and I thought of the cats watching onshore and I said good-bye cat friends, good-bye Cousin Woody, good-bye young life, I am only a little boy and I'm not letting go of this pole, it is not even mine, it's my uncle's. Good-bye school, good-bye Mother and Daddy, don't weep for me, it is a thing in the water cave of my destiny. Yes, I thought all these things in detail while drowning and being pulled rushing through the water, but the sand came up under my feet and the line went slack, the end of the rod was broken off and hanging on the line. When I cranked in the line I saw the hook, a thick silver one, was straightened. The vacancy in the air where there was no fish was an awful thing like surgery in the pit of my stomach. I convinced myself that I had almost had him.

When I stood in the water on solid sand, I began crying. I tried to stop but when I got close to Woody I burst out again. He wanted to know what happened but I did not tell him the truth. Instead I told him I had stepped on an enormous ray and its hook had sliced me.

No.

Yes. I went into briefer sobs.

When we checked my legs there was a slice from an oyster shell, a fairly deep one I'd got while being pulled by the creature. I refused treatment and I was respected for my close call the rest of the day. I even worked in the lie more and said furthermore it didn't much matter to me if I was taken off to the asylum for stingaree children, that was just the breaks. My cousin and the rest of them looked at me anew and with concern but I was acting funny and they must have been baffled.

It wasn't until I was back in the dreaded school room that I could even talk about the fish, and then my teacher doubted it, and she in goodwill with a smile told my father,

congratulating me on my imagination. My father thought
that was rich, but then I told him the same story, the creature so heavy like a truck, the school of porpoises, and he
said That's enough. You didn't mention this when you
came back.

No, and neither did I mention the two cats when I
walked back to shore with Woody and the broken rod. They
had watched all the time, and I knew it, because the both of
them stared at me with big solemn eyes, a lot of light in them,
and it was with these beings of fur then that I entrusted my
confidences, and they knew I would be back to catch the
big one, the singular monster, on that line going tight into
the cave in the water, something thrashing on the end, cel-
ebrated above by porpoises.

I never knew what kind of fish it was, but I would
return and return to it the rest of my life, and the cats would
be waiting to witness me and share my honor.

Carriba

SOMETHING DROPPED, MAYBE A SHOE OUT THERE ON THE polished clay where they've made a path near my south window. There was no sidewalk so they walked a path through the old St. Augustine grass as white trash would do. The woman, Minkle, wants something more with me probably. She'd be out near my window provoking something, that might be what the sound was. I saw her nishy once when she was wet out of the shower but don't think it wasn't offered. She was laughing. I was right under her window. Her brother, the one who killed his father, was in the room beyond her petting the bobcat their horrible mother Blackie had brought up last week. Note the door between their rooms was open. They have a brother named Ebbnut. He stays back in Carriba with Blackie and has fattened within the last year, since the shooting of the father, into a great neckless artillery shell. I would guess Minkle wants my attention now because she is pregnant and the man has quit dating her, that lawyer with cultured looks who used to sit the bench for the university basketball team, in his Volvo.

Or she might want to fight again. Right after that window episode I walked straight in her house past Modock with his bobcat, slammed the door, and beat her up while she was still in the towel. Not badly, but she knew it was due and just took it. Then I came out and sat down, asking Modock what he thought about that, son? He was only now eighteen, stroking that squirming swamp cat he pretended loved him.

Modock wouldn't raise his head.

I say What of it? Get me a beer, you gloomy little saint.

He went and got the beer, bobcat in his arms.

Yes, a good deal was owed me and I liked to call it in from time to time. What began as charity becomes a battle. Life's old tune. Before I could get a good toss of the beer over my lip, however, here comes Minkle in her jogging outfit from her room. Bap, bap, she's into my face with her arms and the beer's flying away one direction, my spectacles the other. I recall Modock rising, get this: so the beer wouldn't get on his bobcat. Sure, into his vow of nonviolence, life-long, after the patricide.

Minkle got me a good sight more than I'd got her. I'm a gentleman, for godsake. Of which, as trash would say, she's hardly no lady. I just took it, looking for my glasses more than even dodging. I let her beat herself out.

You can't hurt me, I said. Then I began laughing. But she was red and nearly weeping in the face.

Hit me some more, wench. Do out this farce. You don't even understand the word, do you?

She began crying then: I'm sorry. I showed myself because I'm so sad, so sad. It wasn't to mean nothing, she spluttered.

You an old man, said Modock.

Take a joke, she said.

I'll eat that pussy right off you, I grinned.

Attaboy she smiled through the tears. We were all familiar again.

Modock looked away. This boy might be a hero, even in the national papers, but by God he was dull. You get this American specimen nowadays that's either shooting some-body or stone boring.

You hear what I said, Modock? That's how old man I am. Put that pussy on my head and wear her down the street like a hat. Hey. I nudged his shoe with mine. You got no honor? I be disrespecting you big sisser. All he could do was look pained and stroke that frowning bobcat, staring out the window as if there were some help out there.

I believe you sisser got some new big bosoms trained out of her from the gym. Got them thigh muscles now. She be a roving clamp, son.

I'd guess the two were separated in age by one of their father's longer penitentiary sentences. Minkle must be thirty-five. In this town, away from Carriba, she had risen in the world. Modock was going nowhere.

He used to wear a python around his neck, down in Carriba. He had a girlfriend too, around his neck when the python wasn't, when I first met him.

Things were much tenderer and more awesome then, and I was a journalist sent down to cover the debris of misery after the killings. Now I am no longer a journalist and am relatively poor. It was the end of my career that way. I had never covered murders and had never worked a story in my home state. Murder is not interesting, friends. Murder is vomit. You may attach a story to it but you are already dishonest to the faces of the dead, in this case Modock's father Henry and two policemen Henry had killed with his shotgun on the town square. I knew I had no place arranging this misery into entertainment, a little *Hamlet* for busybodies and ghouls. Nor could I add my other hyena's worth to our already mocked and derided state, where I lived and worked and hoped. Doesn't this sound noble of me? The fact is I have turned into a geezer and elected alderman of the town here. A booster, even. Around age forty-five there might be a pop and a hiss in your heart, and you are already on your way, a geezer. Nothing is good or like it used to be, not even nookie. A great gabby sadness swarms over you. You are an ancient mariner yanking on the arms of the young. See here, see here.

Modock's distress, sitting there on the couch with the python draped around his neck, his gruesome high school sweetie pressing him to marry her, get a car and a job and some money, threw me into action. Come on, die with us, real close to us, the sweetie and Modock's dreaded mother Blackie might as well be screaming: It's lonesome, come on pretty thing and die with us, snuggle up there. Modock *is* pretty. Put a good sweater on the boy and he's instantly in a movie about the right side of the tracks. I saw him as a freshman here at the university, look of a teenage saint on him—those pained green eyes—first in his family at a college ever. I told him to get out of the place and live near me five hours upstate, in this little gem of a burg. He shocked me by accepting.

Now they're both here, he and Minkle, in that modest brown wooden rental next to me in this white subdivision, mainly red brick and ranchy, of the Eisenhower years. Wide streets and combed curbs with the dogs sleeping away blissfully in their rabbit dreams. Briefly he improved. He had work at the Whirlpool plant and the manager, a pal of mine, gave him a Subaru cockeyed on its frame from an old wreck, so Modock goes forever leftward down the road whichever way he goes. He had his old hound, Beaumont, and I brought him over some books and pictures. His grades were not bad down in Carriba High although he detested the place. Everybody had airs. I noticed even the weather-woman on television seemed to threaten him with airs.

Son, I said, Can't you see the bod on her, those nice smacking lips?

Nobody dressed like that talks about rain, he said.

But the slope, the promise of that hip on her.

You wear you pants around you head.

He was the son of a prisoner released three times to kill again, always pleading self-defense. Always innocent somehow, this man. An altercation on a back porch—somehow the gun discharged, hell of a thing. He wrote songs in prison. His lawyer, a former gubernatorial candidate, showed them to me. Untamed broken heart, Manslaughter One/Miss My Daughter and Tiny Sons. Henry, forever getting a bad deal, just wanted to sing. If he could just quit killing people and get some private lessons. I saw a photograph of him and Modock smiling together, arms across shoulders, a guitar hanging off Henry's neck. It was a good one, not cheap. Henry's hair looked suddenly arisen in oil and hope. Henry and Blackie divorced and remarried several times. She told me she had "been" with Henry the night before his last rampage.

Henry seems to have been one of a very rare breed in whom marijuana, which he used frequently, induced a murderous psychosis. Two young well-built patrolmen had lately been "bothering" him. Or not. Henry had a case of policemen bothering him just about forever. The two cops "shook him down" in front of his friends in a restaurant on the square. He was free of dope. But in a few minutes he walked out to his white camper, perhaps toked-up (although the state toxicology lab pronounced his body free of drugs, Blackie said he was never free of drugs) and set upon the policemen with a twelve-gauge loaded with buckshot. He killed both of them, although there were two bullet holes in the window of the camper, which I examined. Then he went home, where, as the beloved Robert Frost said, they have to take you in. But he went home brandishing the shotgun and wanting to kill everybody. A younger cousin stood in his way and Henry leveled on him. The cousin, a hunched skinny man with homemade tattoos crawling all over his arms (in prison, they use old-timey carbon paper and a needle to do this upon themselves; there's plenty of time), said this to Henry:

Well, Henry, go ahead and do what you have to do.

What you have to do. Imagine. I loved the steel of this, my friends.

I talked to a black policemen about the incident and Henry.

Well, Henry's in heaven now, he said.

In heaven, after killing five men?

He's in heaven.

But I can't figure why he was allowed even on the streets of here, I said.

This earth were not his home.

You forgive him?

There ain't no other choice.

Henry Modock was fifty-three when he died. He had got himself against the wall of the rented barracks compound where they all lived—he sometimes, when in good with Blackie. He continued to rave and to brandish. His son was somehow now in the camper. Henry pointed the gun. Modock rammed him against the wall of the barracks. Henry howled in agony, his last. The boy carried a nine-shot .22 revolver behind his leg. Henry, even in his parlous state, leveled the shotgun one more time. Modock shot him nine times, to death. One guesses it was in essence suicide, this act, but Henry went for the nastier patricide. Consistent with the riot of self-pity forever in the heart of most killers of his stripe. Legacy of the son with bloody hands. Taking you with me, boy. I love you that much. Squeeze on up here for a hug, it's lonesome and deep here.

Why'd you make me shoot you, Daddy? You knew we loved you, said Modock.

This statement went out over the national wire along with the other ghastly events of that afternoon in Carriba. The big slick men's magazine in New York called me. By the time I arrived the bodies were five months old.

Around the room sat Ebbnut, Blackie, Modock and python and high school sweetie, and one of Blackie's sister alcoholics, Pearl from down the road. The women were well into the beer. On the counter of the sink was four pounds of bleeding hamburger defrosting in pink webs over the brown-veined porcelain. Blackie thought I looked Filipino and this idea was hilarious to her and her mate, shrieking away. But the boys moved me. Ebbnut reminded me exactly of an old high school chum who had gone far on the trombone with merry diligence and very small talent. Modock, lean and hungry, startled and sad at the same time if you could tell by his green eyes, was flat-out pretty. He seemed not made for this earth either. He hardly spoke. I withered, already impertinent, an obscenity.

My whole professional life reared up in my mind. I was a hag and a parasite. I was to be grave and eloquent over their story, these people I would not have spat at unless three people had been murdered. They were to get nothing. I was to get fame and good bucks, provided I was interesting. A great sick came on me. Already I was looking at leaner but better years.

Minkle was not in the house. I believe she was currently over in Hattiesburg failing at something menial. Her ex-husband was in prison. Her grandfather, Blackie's Pa, had been in prison. I had already seen him while tracing the new whereabouts of the Modocks. He was a little man out cutting a huge lawn around a tiny box of a house. *You know: we've had our troubles,* he said. He was worried about Blackie's drinking problem. Blackie was currently worried about the $15,000 insurance on "my husband's" life. She was also screaming at the police, who would not return the clothes of "my husband." For some reason she wanted back the clothes he had on when he was shot. When something was owed Blackie, I noted she struck the formal tone "my husband."

I saw them five times and at no time did anybody commiserate with the families of the dead policemen. They listened to a police-band radio for home entertainment, even still. I noticed police-band radios were the hottest item at every pawnshop in town. A running battle with the police was a fact as manifest as wallpaper. I'd noticed the same about some bikers in Pensacola I wrote about. Take away the harassment and dogged persecution of the police and the folks had little cause to exist. I suspected Blackie was a looker at one time but she was fast turning dry, blotched, and yellow, with dark teeth through which she issued this astounding promise: *When I get my husband's insurance money I'm gettin' me a good gun. We need us a good gun.*

I nearly dropped my pencil. Modock was silent, as usual, with his sweetie pressing up to him, whispering about money, job, and car. Modock had a deep curious thing going with his ma, as most of us do, but these were Mississippi criminal Irish and among them Mama Love often kills, one way or the other. I began glaring at Blackie as the likely source of it all, or much of it. She caught on to this, got drunker, and I left with her spitting a much meaner and more poisonous laughter, as if I'd just kicked over her rock and

she was lying all twisted and naked beyond my heels. Among
the dispossessed you find an insane loyalty in family mem-
bers that does not exclude murder of their own. *Go ahead,
Henry, and do what you have to do.*

I told Modock if he stayed here he would die. He
should live in my town and give the line beginning with him
another whole chance.

Blackie, way in the background, had somehow heard
me. I heard the shriek.

Nevertheless, in two weeks, he was at my door, behind him Blackie in a smoking Pontiac belonging to her mate
up front who was too drunk to drive. Little Ebbnut was in
the backseat with his kind smile. The car filthy with oil and
dust over mud. You could barely read the tag when they
turned and left. Pearl River County. Modock had said only,
I'm here. Blackie called out the words that still rang, in her
hag's shriek, *I see where you live! See where you live, Filipino!*

I asked Modock, there with his bag and hound Beaumont on my front porch, where his sweetheart was. She'd
barely left his hip when I was in Carriba.

Put her away from me.

And came right here.

Like you said. Get a new life.

It was June and I rented the house next door, a lesser
brown box in this old exurb, not ranchy at all. More chicken-
houselike but squared into four rooms inside as if by a child
with a ruler. My wife was soon muttering, no surpise, since
she's from mother stock who's narrowed the world down to
one gallstone. But neveryoumind, I took her off to Paris, gave
her a Gold card, put us up in a fancy hotel that was Gestapo
headquarters during the Occupation, and climbed her like
an alp while she grabbed the curtains. She came back drip-

ping with history and stayed actually mute and tender toward the world for a couple weeks. Thing that saves us is that the house is enormous and I don't see her for days. She deeply resented having to cook the one night for Modock, and I would pay for it, I knew. Please, please, punish me with silence, I begged her with my eyes. She panted back to her great leisure room where she has three-hour phone conversations with her kin about how many people they have told off today, barks of victory spilling out now and then like canned soundtrack. Great God, and here I was already going from upper to flat middle class, in some fear. They gave me a class in journalism at the university. It was hard being smooth and unneedy when I applied, but I had a name and I'd once witnessed for a prof there who stayed out of jail.

I was eating with my cronies at a downtown pizza and pasta bar when something hit me hard in the back of the head. Then I heard the pop of a shoe, a sneaker on the plank floor, and saw a body in a jumpsuit hastening away, with girl hair on top of it. This was Minkle. I'd never seen her before and here she's popped me among friends in a town absolutely strange to her. She turned, about twenty feet away, not looking even faintly like Blackie or the rest of them, and waved as if we'd been bosom chums since rocks and water. I had no idea who she was, but she hollered over.

I'm here now. Come on in the house. Don't be a stranger.

As if I could sense who she was and she knew I could. And she was right. I was baffled a little by the blow to the head, but she couldn't be anybody else.

Soon afterward, it was at Kroger's, where I enjoy watching others' wives, a hard rod came in my ribs at an aisle-turn. This hurt. It was Minkle at the end of a mop who'd rammed me. She had a broad smile on.

Uh-oh! Watch out now!

I was in misery and didn't smile at all. I don't think I said anything, just covered my ribs with my hands where it hurt, seriously hurt. Then she was gone, with a giggle.

There was a vast chemical spill in Carriba years ago, from a plant that packed up and left. Downtown, a man walked the streets wearing bright universal orange tape around his knees. He said it was to keep alligators away. A policeman I spoke to over the phone told me that the town was run top to bottom by a conspiracy of homosexuals. Henry Modock had wandered freely here. Several claimed he was the nicest man they'd ever met, almost. The town drug dealer worked from a roadhouse and was straight out the worst man I'd ever looked at, a grim, giant-stomached muskrat with no shirt and enormous fat red feet in sandals. He was holding the youngest of his infants while his wife raised an ungodly din back in the living quarters. The man may have been furtive but it could have done him no good. He wasn't even a modern criminal. He belonged in the line of psychotic white trash straight from the days of Mike Fink. Feet dyed by the pirate river. I heard he was sly and stayed out of prison because "he done good turns now and then for the police." Yet he was arrested within the week on big drug charges. Everybody knew what he did and where he was. You'd get directions to Benny Harp, the drug dealer. Sure, the town had its mansions and fine people. A former governor had built a Spanish mansion here. I spoke to two of these prosperous good boys. Both of their wives had gone mad within a week of each other. Another told me he deeply feared the ocean. It was an hour and a half away. Yet another shot his father-in-law out of a tree stand, thinking he was a "wolfbear." Straight across the Mississippi River in Louisiana was a north-south rough rectangle seventy miles long besotted by petrochemicals for generations. It had the highest incidence of cancer in the nation.

So now Minkle. It was not clear for a while whether she'd moved in with Modock to save him or herself.

She had a job at Wal-Mart and had begun wearing hosiery. She came up on that northern path they had made in the yard, almost under my window, to get in her car, a plain Ford given over by her prisoner ex-husband. She had a clean face and new shoes. Then she ran in the streets in the evenings, with a radio in her head, just like a coed. I saw her disappear down the hill, all shoe soles and butt, in her jogging Speedo. She was getting an over-all suntan, perhaps at a gym, and in my indifference I watched the woman change from plain to outright fetching. In my patient geezer lechery I did admire her. She was a good big sister to Modock. The place was cleaner and there were flowers around. The hound got washed once a week and began to appear sleek and noble, with a nice leather collar and vaccination tag on him. I think even his posture improved. He would stare out at the street like a perfectly adapted suburban philosopher, rich in black and tan.

I was out getting the paper in the drive early on a Saturday, didn't see it, and bent down to a bush where it might be hidden. She was in the bush and whapped me upside the head with my own rolled newspaper.

Lookin' for somethin', neighbor?

You're a rough one, aren't you?

Can't you take it?

I reached over and yanked down her Speedo bra, then slapped her mildly.

Good morning, I said.

She set herself right, not as shocked as she might be and a smile coming up.

I brought you some rent. She had money in her hand. I looked at it and was puzzled, then all at once touched. It was green and black cash, somewhat wet in her palm, twenties I guess. You could feel the hours in it, the earning, like the money of a kid at a lemonade stand.

When you get on your feet—, I started.

We on our feet.

Very well.

I almost didn't take it. Maybe I wanted to own them a bit longer.

Modock's not going to college, is he? I said to her.

No. But I am. He's swore nonviolence. Too many persons around give him trouble.

What does he do after work over there?

I have to open a big can of whupass on bro now and then, get him out of that stare, not eatin'.

You beat up Modock?

I get his attention. What he did, there's not many like him in the world, you know. But he's got to unbrood himself and move on.

There was a man in town who had killed his mother. Her death was a drunken accident in a car he drove through police roadblocks with his mother, eighty, as a passenger. She was thrown from the car. After his arrest they watched him for suicide. Only a mattress in a windowless room at the hospital. We all expected him to go to prison. It was the worst thing one could do, this matricide, and prison would not touch the guilt, we imagined. I suppose we expected him to crumble and seek hell. But mourning has its limits. I would guess there might come a day when you do not murder yourself with grief, you have become a part of it. You are the definition of grief, and you keep moving, a monster beyond atonement, a shadow of guilt on the wall to your neighbors. His sister wrote the judge a moving letter. The man did no prison time. He is simply doing time there in the grocery store. People, including me, do not know how to look at him even when we say hello. He is the permanent bottom line of horror, maybe even another breed.

I wondered should this man and Modock meet. Should they form a rare club.

But Modock worked and came home. He was looking thin and sorry. They told me he was neither good nor bad at work. His boss said this odd thing: *Modock doesn't want to know or remember things. Every day it's like he just first came on the job.* He didn't mind being shouted at. He never laughed at a joke.

They had been in town several months before Modock missed a day of work. I noted his leftward auto at the curb around eleven and went over. The house was dark and Modock sat on a far chair in boxer underwear with a bar of light across his eyes. The eyes seemed out on stalks away from the grave and emaciated face. They seemed cracked with light inside. Modock had become a haint of his former self. He scared me. I got him a glass of water and felt heat coming off his body from his fingers. He said he had been throwing up a little. The old television was not on, only the hum of the refrigerator was heard, aggressive, a raw and odd tune here.

Black girls, he said. Two black girls at work found out what I did with my daddy. They said I had taken the hell from him and now the hell was in me. I was hell and I was in hell and there was forever a mark on me, which I already knew.

Now you've just talked yourself into a case of the flu, boy.

I don't have the flu.

Your pa was begging you to shoot him. Like he was on fire and couldn't stand it.

I was doing all right until somebody said it, them girls.

He wanted company in hell but don't give it to him, nor to your mother.

I'm not having a new life.

Sink then. Call your mama and get another lease on the old shit.

Blackie in fact had been calling me for a while, always something, but unbearable when she was drunk. The police would not give back "my husband's" camper or his clothes or Modock's gun, either. She'd go down and raise hell at the station. But now she wanted to sell her life story for a great deal of money. I would write it. I'm afraid not, I told her. She then told me I'd better watch out for Modock. No, I won't, I said.

In a week I saw the car over there, rammed up to the porch. Ebbnut was around, assisting something with a burred tail, moving it into the house. This was the bobcat, still muddy from the swamps near Carriba. Modock wasn't moving out as I'd thought. They'd brought more of Carriba to him. Poor Ebbnut was even more swollen. Some say depression among the poor shows up instantly as fat. The boy was not only neckless but nigh to growing another face across. Blackie, of course, was lean in her alcoholism. Already she had married another wretch, a man who stayed behind the wheel. Modock had had three other stepdads while Henry was in prison. This one didn't even cause a ripple. He seemed merely frozen in the act of valet. Imagine the bite of such love as he could wrest at evening from each day's journey.

I suddenly thought of my own case. I had wanted a great woman but then I was not a great man, always in this swoon of brooding. Even my aldermanship was a stretch. I did not care that much.

Frozen at the wheel of this my old Mercury of a body, driven up on foreign shores, weary of the music from my ancient radio, beyond me barely intelligible voices in odd rooms, an eye out for the leap of the unexpected. It was ever thus. I was never firmly native to anywhere. Yet ravenous for the unexpected. Half amazed that others even bother to carry on.

I at last danced with Minkle. I saw her alone at that discotheque two art queers began with one's grandfather money. It was an instant failure and I felt sorry for the fellows. They thought a revival would be all the rage. But not here. Only Minkle and a few others came. She was dancing with one of the owners under great speakers full of Donna Summer and the Bee Gees. There was a billiard table lit in the corner and big dying ferns of all nations set around. Big pulse, a raised platform for styling where sad queers offered themselves up to the lonely passion of the Pet Shop Boys. One grabbed a silver fireman's pole and expressed himself around it, dying as if rammed by heaven.

I walked over and popped her a stout one against the head. Drunk and in blue jeans, I was not recognized at first. But then she held her head and smiled. At last I was Bob Bubb, famous old son of her orbit. I was down in the bottoms with the boys, lanterns and dogs on the hunt for a screaming bobcat, or *painter* as they called them down Carriba way.

Oh oh you're so extreme I want to take you home with me.

I went flailing around the beat, another sad old married like most of the queers in this town.

We danced something out, god knows what, but I was earnest, earnest, wanting out and up so badly. All this weight we get in time. It isn't that childhood was any better, it's that it was so much lighter.

I whispered to her I wanted to be crucified upside down like Saint Peter over her naked form. Of course she didn't hear me. Or maybe she did. When the tune stopped she tore up my hair with her hands and cracked me across the back of the head with an elbow. My hair was ruined and flared-out like Stan Laurel's, I saw in the mirror. My fly was unbuttoned and Minkle corrected this. She had on a tie-dyed T-shirt. I had felt sorry for her, out there with that gay fellow. Give her a break and let her dance with an alderman and former journalist. I was a worthy, many respected me. She was rising.

Now she had a job at the university television station. She helped produce programs for welfare mothers that educated them for the mainstream, a government project with a heartwarming acronym attached run by a shady parasite who kept a car phone in his bass boat. The sparse crowd of collegiates out on the floor reminded me she was taking several classes.

You've done well, Minkle, with your talents here, I said.

You mean barely high school?

I mean the Carriba situation. A place develops its own luck, you know. A family from Carriba lived near me when I was growing up. Terrible things were always happening to them. Car wrecks, cancer, fires. Boat explosions. Saying all this made me sober, I swear. There was something true about it that cut through nine drinks and brought on a brightly lit melancholy.

You know it wasn't but the one thing, she said.

The one thing?

That Modock was *worth* coming here for a fresh start. Well I went on and interpreted that I might be worth it too. You gave us that.

Modock doesn't seem—

Modock is dying, man. He's either going to make it or he's not. I believe he almost has to die and get better. Or not. I know it.

He could talk to a doctor, I guess. Tell it to a group, I said.

No. One of those days one of them would say to him: I know how you feel. Then I'd go up there and tear into them and want our money back. It's in the blood, man. My mother Blackie beat up several doctors.

When I left the disco, walking, I was drunk again and melancholy both. I wandered to the front window of an auto parts dealer chum of mine, as if he'd be open. He was marrying the ex-wife of a rich doctor. I wanted to explain to him how important friendship was in this cold universe. I wanted to explain to him that what television and bad American movies had done was to make us doubt that others even existed except as a shadow play. That virtual reality and cyberspace would complete the job. That you could not be sure that you were at your own father's funeral. Or think the woman squirming under you was only good if it would make a good movie. Or doubt that there had been any football on a live field because there was no replay. As some GI in his first firefight in Vietnam was supposed to have hollered out: Where's the soundtrack!? That the poisonous excuse for all bad on television was that: But it's *true*. I was hammering on the glass doors, wanting my chum to be in and talk this over. When I turned around, in front of the grocery store in his apron with meat stains on it, there under the fluorescent lights having a cigarette, was the man who'd killed his mother.

I rushed home and woke up my wife. I pulled the gown back down to her waist and gave her a massage, in terrible grief. We have to love each other, I said. Even if we don't want to, we have to. Cling to a buoy even though half of it's shot away.

I love you too, she said. Leave me be, midnight poet.

But I was back in the disco the next night as if to complete something unfinished. That '70s music. During Vietnam I was in Korea in the army around the 38th parallel. In bell-bottoms, beads, and bandanna wrap, a buddy and I used to give the finger to the Koreans across the valley who rolled out artillery from their caves every morning. That was some bad dope. We had been listening to the bulletproof Hendrix.

For the longest while even fewer people were coming in. Some of them were even more pathetic than the other evening. I sensed they were *trying* to be queer but hadn't the moves. I loved it, racing through vodka martinis and huge onions.

I waited and waited and waited, staring at the baroque mirror at a man who was dwindling into something else. I would bark out involuntarily sometimes, as if with Tourette's syndrome, saying No! No! Perhaps I had taken on some of Modock's grief, was now a barking dummy for the killer son. I hadn't meant to, but I kept erupting, as if somebody was there accusing me. Finally the whap on the back of the head came, but not so hard, even some tenderness in it. I turned and it was Minkle, but she was accompanied by the long-haired lawyer, young and blond, pretty vacant in the face.

She put her hands around my neck and dragged me to her. Next I knew my head was turned and she was pouring a kiss down my mouth, a tongue in there. It was ten years since I'd had a kiss like this. My wife used to be good at it in her throes. But hell, I knew what Minkle was up to. She was kissing a man of importance to mark the fact that she had classy friends.

During the week, she'd get in his car evenings and give me a pout as she nestled in his Volvo. I'd hang at the window there. She meant some kind of low irony I didn't understand. I wasn't angry or jealous. I just despised the obvious deal being struck here. The urgency of her rise, the flat coy look on the ex-jock now Volvo lawyer.

It is the sadness of Modock's old hound I want to address here. In the next few days, displaced by the bobcat, he lay next to the steps in full mourning. Hounds are mournful anyway, but he was in clear further distress. He even came over to visit and get some affection, as he'd never done before. In his eyes were both the mourning of the world and the unexpected torture of Modock's neglect.

Inside, the bobcat was all cleaned up. Modock made much over it. Pretending it was getting all homey. Any fool could see its eyes looking out for every crack of egress. Modock was back at work and may have been a little ruddier. The few visits I made made me angrier.

Your mama can't be here so she wants you stroking that cat, which is her, which is Carriba, I told him. What about Beaumont?

He didn't answer.

Beaumont's not wild or mean enough, is he? He ain't got that spitting beauty to him, what? You suffering all over that cat, stroking away, running round after its poopoo. This makes quite a story. Only you can't see it.

I'm not a story. I'm people, he said.

Well, months, and we went on. Minkle ran home glistening, a bit more stylish every week. She picked up fast, only she was copying things a bit young for her, like two bows in the hair, blue jeans with the knees out. Once I felt for her so much, watching her that way, I started crying a little. And I had never stopped the involuntary barks, the looking around as if there were somebody there on my case.

She got pregnant, the guy stopped coming by, and she showed me her nookie at the window. She cheered up some after the fight. But the hound Beaumont now was emaciated and weak with grief. Modock was a killer but he was not cruel, that I knew of. I took over the hound. Can you believe it? The hound brought the wife and me closer together. She made over it, gave Beaumont special scraps, and he got some hope in his eyes. It had been ages since she'd nursed anything. My word what you find just stumbling around. Both the hound and I were getting some, with wild and tender goodwill.

At the school was a little man who had followed the civil rights struggle and written several books about it, a white man. He had a name and esteem, but in the hall I attacked him for being a civil rights junkie with his eye on the main chance, a part of the modern university industry where all the grants and prizes were. I accused him of living off the grief of better men. That he was a tick. At the end of this, with several students around, I began barking, No! No!

They let me go.

Amazing but that very afternoon I came across a stanza from Charles Simic that buried right into me, although I never read poetry. Simic had been on campus, a friend urged the book on me, a page blew open at my window.

I tell you, I was afraid. A man screamed
And continued walking as if nothing had happened.
Everyone whose eyes I sought avoided mine.
Was I beginning to resemble him a little?
I had no answer to any of these questions.
Neither did the crucified on the next corner.

Even so I was not doing well. I reread the stanza, even more afraid, and regarded the stack of letters on my desk. I should have been flattered, these magazines begging me to come back to their world. Assignments in grave astounding places all over the world. I had almost nothing left in savings. Yet I felt unable to move.

I went over to Modock's angrier than ever and didn't hear the protest inside before I yanked out the screen door and the bobcat was through my legs. Modock might be weak but he was fast, up the hill of the house across the street, a big hill, right after the creature. But beyond the house, I knew, was a valley of deep kudzu, old tall stricken trees, and this went on for a half mile. I could hear Modock's screams, and then his weeping, like a tot who's lost everything, over the hill. It was an hour before he came back, and he was ripped bloody by thorns, and green at the knees where he'd been crawling.

So he got sicker again. I was the villain. He became crazed, sitting by the phone all hours after work. He expected somebody to call. About the bobcat. Some person who's a fair person, he told me. Minkle and I stared on, horrified.

This can't go on, I said. I'd never seen Minkle, the jogging optimist, in real despair. But now she was square in it, all pregnant and stunned.

So it could not go on, could not.

I made a couple of calls that night, in my own study, after reading the Simic again. My people with your people, the business. At suppertime the next evening I told Modock and Minkle to be present and ready. Midnight.

His name was Ferdinand but he was called Ferd. A few minutes before midnight he took off his apron very positively. I saw hardly a hint of doubt or even concern in his eyes. He had cut some flowers that were waiting in the refrigeration bin where they sold them. He tamped a few Clorets into his mouth, and I could tell his hair had been recently combed. Ferd wasn't a handsome man, but he had a good smile. The thing that shocked me was that he thought I had been friendlier to him these couple years than I was aware of. He counted on me as a pal, just by my minimal greetings. I felt very unworthy but this didn't last long. Too many days now, I had been a barking worm, grimness wrapped around my head like my old bandanna of Korea. It was time to move and do.

We were admitted in the front door by Minkle. I looked over at Modock in the chair, so skinny and petrified with fear.

This is Ferd, the guy who killed his mother, I announced him.

Ferd held the flowers, and I swear, *became* handsome in his delight.

Sure, I'll marry you. Seen you 'bout, he said.

Now look. I want the three of you to mix and talk. I'll be off months doing stuff I've got to. Get in there, and by fuck, get along.

Either way you want it, I'm there, said Ferd. Have the baby or not I'll love it like it's my own, said Ferd. I've many times thought I could be a powerful father.

Well, said Minkle, looking at me. This don't seem like it's in . . . very good taste.

Taste? *Taste,* I swore at her.

Even so, the look she was giving Ferd, ignoring me, was not a bad one.

Snerd and Niggero

Mrs. Niggero was in there with Mr. Snerd on the couch. She had her dress folded back on her thighs with her gift out to Snerd, who was minutely rolling the hem onward so as to roll it even more to her globes' bottoms. Then his rolling goes even more up her so her dress was as a rolled flag around her neck and one cup of her brassiere was hanging off her left globe. Mr. Snerd liked her earlobes even better than that, though, now after these long years. He has his fingers up to them and nicks them and fondles them as Mrs. Niggero consumed him up to his navel to her chin, even mashing her freckles there, and sobs around his fundament. Mrs. Niggero didn't want this at first because she was married to another man, Cornelius.

But she had been doing this eighteen years with Snerd whom she can't not love in another way. So Snerd played with her ears and croons to her while she sobs preparing him for the inevitable though now somehow sad primary entrance. She squeezed her eyes blind and he with resignation pushed in amidperson, a little deaf with grief and wild comfort. Then she smiled the more now. Snerd saw her smile, too, as she delays the primary act, withdraws herself in beauty, and plunges down amid his person, soon with her eyes happily on him above her stuffed mouth where she moves in jazz with the clutches of her throat, because she cannot help her loves and now she must slow the fever down, not bring off Snerd's pathos and ultimatum too quickly. Because her joy is growing only as fast as a spring garden while Snerd is the tropical bamboo.

This thing has been described ever since Snerd beheld her face, in a chilly bank, over her legs bare, tan, and cool like those eggs from certain hens, while on her feet were flat petite Roman sandals, midheeled, the straps of them over the curve of her instep on the feet above the toes, which pitched Snerd's eyes upwards to her childish belted waist and high bosom, under cloth of a wildflower print, apricot. Snerd was in pain for her immediately, sweating on his checks written sloppily to him by bohemians and the old. He never afterwards collected himself, but was a man alive hardly anywhere else but near her: he had no will, but dragged his heart and blue loins through ruined hours away from the reach of her.

She was married but he stood in her lawn and watched her eat with her husband Cornelius in a yellow room, then walked into her flowers and amongst her high azalea bushes, near the windowsill, below which he ground himself on a whitened plank, calling in a whisper.

Now Mrs. Niggero—Nancy—sighed and Snerd retired from her lips, then went like a slave at them again. She met him with a luxury of stroke in her cunny and pulled him in way out of his depth so Snerd was almost anxious as with his waist jerked down a well, but safe, his balls would not go further, and the two of them settled into the planes of full criminal love, pulling each the other's organ from its aim and both losing; something like a pilgrim running back and forth through the doorway of a shrine, welcomed then ejected.

Mrs. Niggero in an agony of pleasure gave birth to root and Snerd commenced his spurts with a prayer. She, all gone, pleaded quietly for his final drops. Robert Snerd, married blithely in indifference himself, was already jealous of her minutes away from him with Cornelius.

They were ashamed shortly afterwards, gathering the old clothes on for the miserable attritions demanded by the clock, in a flat horror of the zombies such as count, hasten small distances, and get mean-eyed over the matter of a nickel in the bank where Snerd first saw her. Each time they were a little incredulous such raw worship had overcome them, for eighteen years. With a terrible clasp of the other, they fled apart. Mrs. Niggero wept and had a limp. Snerd was grim in the years of his week until he saw her again but nonetheless forcing his shadow to the outer window of the bookstore he owned. He looked in on his staff, smart girls nearly devout in their errands; here and there a customer, a browser, wanting someone else's life; the books themselves, the thousands of titles grown alien and faintly nauseating to him. He had rather warm his mind vainly in thought about his valiant hot seed still within the treacherous loins of Nancy Niggero, now in her married home. Her husband would now at seven P.M. be sitting across the room from her, looking at her although pretending interest in the television book. Mr. Niggero, hardly more than a curved backbone with a damp shirt hung on it. She would be forced into the worst role, managing her contempt by the second. An eruption might mean the end of the world.

But Snerd was in error. Nancy loved this silent drooping man deeply and burned like a penitent, always intent to sense his needs, which were few, in happy submission. Niggero watched her slyly too, and with an urge to haul goods to her feet and roll in them like a dog, then next day wag off to his work as city attorney, provided a desk and an old-fashioned clerk's eyeshade he imagined touched him with romance in accuracy; and the briefs of fretting gnatlike spite. He for twenty-seven years had been driven pale and near emaciated by them, but his eyes still glowed with a beautiful near-insane gray like a wolf's with his nose raised for a feast six counties away and hearing—eyes and ears at attention to the far-off. He was not a dog, neither just the curved spine under a sweated shirt, a mere hanger for expensive broadcloth shirts and paisley neckties seen in *Gentleman's Quarterly*. There was about him still an extremely nervous happiness of search and a small glee that he was not nearly close to its end yet. On the edge of his tongue was the appeal "Please stomp my grapes!" now for several years. Stomp my grapes. He did not know why, quite, nor was the appeal constantly there, and he knew every minute of the day it was inappropriate and scandalous.

Cornelius Niggero, because of his name partly, had never done a thing inappropriate yet and felt always shy under the odd banner of this title. He was almost bowled over by the weight of his name, enough. Even more so than by the vicious tedium of his work for the city. These days there seemed a parental or student suit at least once a week in the school system. But he loved Nancy too much to announce out loud about stomp my grapes please. He was impatient until she had everything she wished, which, as with himself, was not very much at all. She had the large clean house, splendid clothes, and ready means of travel to anywhere she wanted.

Nancy Niggero, however, a clean and even reverent person, was frugal and a creature of not much whim. Even though in Niggero's eyes an authentic aristocrat, she was plain and definite in her speech and not partial to the vaguely depressed chatter of that class at all, even with a nice woman's college in the East and European travel behind her. She was very north Mississippian. Of all beings she seemed to him the one most certain why she was born and went about her days as if fetched by a quiet honorable master, a call from both firmament and fundament. She astonished him and was his saint. He could never comprehend why she had married him, because he knew he was dulling and only pulled forth per diem by a fog of uncertain promise, only solid when he thought of seeing her once again and already grateful, his tongue hardly restrained from lupine rapture. Even now looking at her he could see her again tomorrow night in a different softer blouse perhaps. He could see her mailing her poems at the post office and nearly wept for her lack of success in that work, although she reviewed every rejection with a sly grin of defeat. In every other thing in life she was accepted. This was a fine mystery to her. Niggero would have cut half his finger off if she could have only one triumph. He defended her with an inner rage. It seemed highly relevant here, what he had read in some book of inspiration months ago: "When a finger points at the moon, the imbecile looks at the finger." He remembered this as Chinese. Nancy seemed suddenly even more lovely as Chinese herself to him—radiant, calm, and stoical.

In her nightgown in low light, her wet hair bound back by a scarf, she was a wrenching vision. Niggero could almost scream to her, "Stomp my grapes!" *Please,* asked her without sound, as she passed against the moony glass of the front door and he could hear the rush of her slippers, see her legs move her gown. It would fairly put him to sleep in admiration. When she made an uncivil stomach sound, he blamed it on the dog. She was such a wife that Niggero felt selfish and had an impulse to share her with something large and hungry, which he did in a manner when they ate with the mayor and his wife and he watched the *both* of them with their helpless eyes on her.

Even in winter Niggero sweated too much. He was more noxious to himself than anyone else. A grim fever was on him. It was necessary he put himself in slow motion ever since the advent of midlife in order to prevent the moisture from running into his socks. His shirt wet and rank, he had to change each day at noon. There was a space with a mirror in his closet at city hall in which he saw his beaded face, same as in the air force years ago, blurred since, quite a bit, though not lean as it should be: Italian bloodhound, semitic without distinction, nose made for the dense odors of southern Europe and blown up by them. But the blazing wolf's eyes in the center—if his eyes could see his eyes—two beacons on a saddle. He often broke wind with a great searching hook of sound, poisoning his closet just beyond the mayor's secretary at her desk, and emerged red with scandal and blindness. His lungs seemed too narrow and gunked in a residue of half a year of menus. Through the window in back he saw the rubble of the rear yard one late afternoon. He was drawn to it suddenly, the glass and brick fragments and shrubweed, so he opened the window and crawled out into it. Here was his true neighborhood.

It was exile he deserved in his undeserving existence, and he squatted in it, arguing with the deer fleas and chummy ticks already on his hands. Since thirty he had been aware of being nearly dead and was shocked when anybody, even the city in legal trouble, needed him. Then he scrambled up and walked around the front of the ancient and chalky red brick city hall. The grand doorway ennobled him. He felt halfway a man about town, certified; at least a unit of the edifice, a brick with a nose. Some bustling town music, such as that in an old movie from the late forties, seemed to announce itself around him. Niggero went leaping back to his job. A hired extra, lost in the republic.

Robert Snerd watched him without contempt, just then. Moved in fact to charity, feeling old and the butt of something himself, he looked down at the clean pavement at another blind decade, gray with infinitesimal holes like the concrete walk. Snerd invoked another memory of Niggero, once when he saw him alone watching his enormous shepherd run down the hill of a ditch near the baseball stadium. Niggero looked very foreign and diminished by the healthy players out tiny on the practice field. Snerd was lost in compassion, then bewildered by a sudden respect for the fellow, so made for treachery, like an idol of betrayal, there scrambling down for his dog, stubborn in a culvert.

When Mrs. Niggero died of an acutely quadraplegical muscular thing that roared into her almost overnight, three years later, Robert Snerd thought for a while that the formality of his public inexpression of grief had damaged his true sorrow. He had never wept, only stared. He could not wink out even a drop, even missing Nancy and seeing her whole, in sandals only, her bold chest and pubic darkness strutted out for him as a display of promised bounty. This was a posture she had never struck in real life. Here she was whispering something with a sly smile on her, and holding a sheaf of her unpublished poems behind a thigh as if to promise even rarer pleasures if he could help her get them published, a thing, with his considerable connections to small elegant presses, he had never been able to accomplish in real life. In fact her only public poem was the one Cornelius had chosen for her gravestone in quotation marks. To Snerd, this was unfortunate. It was a poem crisp but woozy at the same time, so sentimental it almost washed out her eminence in flesh and belied her highly arousing natural voice, a music of the most moving classical resignation. But then as the weeks passed, he knew he was doing no act for the town and propriety but was an utter stone bastard. He simply was not feeling that much. He had let everything of her but the merely photographic go, entirely. This thing terrified him. All those thousands of books around him thirty years and what they had made him was a monster insensate as a concrete city lion.

He could not help himself, and telephoned Niggero in three days.

"Cornelius! We, so many of us, knew but didn't say what was right to her and to you when she was here with us. She was such a delightful creature. The disadvantage of this pretty bustling little town is it has shut us up and let us take beautiful, beautiful things for granted. Like Nancy. Like you, Robert. A queen, her unassuming . . . prince! Yes, prince behind her! No fanfare. Then she's gone. I need to talk about her with you, I've got to. Let's go somewhere . . . off . . . and chat. I need you, I have to talk."

"You need *me??*" Niggero was astounded. "Well, sure. I've not talked much either. Fucking head for numbers, briefs, stuck in my tongue. I neglected her."

As if nowhere near the town would do for this business, Snerd drove Niggero up near Iuka to a grand reservoir of the Tennessee River, green and rocky like another region of the world completely. They stood at the end of a pier that was condemned to progress, being merely wooden. It was a matter of the heart to Snerd, who had loved the place twenty years and more.

Now a solid rocket fuel plant, with its visiting executives of all nations, had bought the park and was turning it into a convention resort and would put concrete piers with elegant slips on the water.

For the two older men, who were bored, both of them, by talks of the apocalypse ever since they had been born, this was their apocalypse and both sensed it, as Niggero got angry along with Snerd talking about the destruction of the old wooden pier and all things of their youth.

"I knew her too in a way," Snerd began about Nancy. "I sensed she was private, but there were little secrets she gave away I've never told anybody about. I thought you'd like to hear them."

"Very much. I idolized her too much to even know her, I have to confess. There's a strength in me she left behind. I can't even name it. There's been less grief than I imagined, and I've been guilty about it."

In the next fifteen years, before Snerd died—buried promptly by his wife, who remarried avidly and with great whorish avarice a widowed doctor of their acquaintance—it was said the two men enjoyed a friendship such as had hardly been known in the whole north part of the state, and even up through Memphis.

Ned Maxy,
He Watching You

MANY, TOO MANY, DAYS, NED MAXY HAD STARED OUT A window weeping, fasting, and praying, in his way. In character of both the drunkard and the penitent he had watched life across the street. Now in a healthier time, arising to his work at early hours, he labored at his front window table, peering out now and then at a world that spoke back to him. Not loudly and not a lot, but some. Over the white board fence he'd just painted, and through the leaping wide leaves of his muscadine arbor, he spied shyly like a stranger in town. He put his right arm out to the west and something quiet but with a shape happened so that he could feel hills rolling down to the continental delta of the Mississippi, feel the country under his forearm and elbow. The satisfaction of this almost frightened him.

The woman who left in her uniform every morning at a quarter to eight was a paramedic. In the awful '70s Maxy had sworn to hundreds in saloons that he wanted most of all to be a paramedic. This was a lie, one of the great pieties he used to drown out the fact that he wanted most of all to drink more without consequences. Maxy did not know the paramedic woman but he watched her through a pair of opera glasses he had bought at a Hot Springs pawnshop from a man broken in the '70s who sat with his crutches beside him and lit up unfiltered Luckies that made him retch. Maxy at the horse races had dumbly glassed the horses, the tiny men, and some high-style women bred to the sport, wanting to eat and plunder them.

In his late forties the lifetime monster of lust had released him, first time since he was eleven, just as the lifetime monster of drink had released him four years ago. He still did not know precisely what accounted for it, but it was a deep lucky thing, now that he was able to see the woman paramedic across the street leaving for work and comprehend her happiness without him. He looked on in high admiration, goodwill, and with no panic. She was engaged to a wide man with a crew cut who came out with her to the doorway on his big white legs, in Bermuda shorts, and embraced her, seeing his love off in the cool of the morning. Maxy applauded their love. Maxy had been in love this way twice in his life. As the dawn broke through a gray fog that morning, he saw it making the day for their happiness. He recalled the stupid rapture and had no advice for them at all.

He had spoken to the woman only once, told her she looked good in her uniform, all ready to fly in a helicopter and bounce away in mercy on her high-topped black leather sneakers. She had the voice of a country girl, the kind of girl who had soothed his old man dying in the hospital at age eighty-seven. The old fellow had got rich in the city but loved the country much better, and the nurse was a sweet comfort at the last. Maxy liked that this country girl had the moxie to fly in a machine that would have terrified many hillbillies, and he told her so. Even from a hundred yards he could see her go shy, head of blond hair lowered to look at her own eminent bosom—for which he was not required anymore to dream in impossible lechery—having an unexpected compliment sail out to her from a man who didn't need anything, here in the late cool of a summer morning.

She answered some way he couldn't make out, in a whisper, a country whisper of thanks good beyond form.

This whole exchange would not have been possible even three months ago, when in his mind he would have been teaching her the needs of his famished world, her body a naked whirlwind of willing orifices, smiling all the while like the prince of liars at her.

The whisper too had fetched back for him his old mighty friend Drum, lately a suicide. Drum was a practicing Christian, one of maybe four selfless men Ned Maxy had known in life, brought low by pain and anxiety after a heart attack. He was cut off from good work and high spirits and could not go on, they said. Drum was the only whispering drunkard Maxy knew. Through all thunders and the '70s, he had never raised his voice.

He killed himself in the bathroom of a double-wide mobile home he rented from a preacher who lamented to the police: Now poor Drum can't ever go to heaven. But he had been tidy in the bathtub there with the large-caliber pistol, much appreciated.

His drinking buddy Drum's whispers of encouragement, his pleading to Maxy that he was a man who must respect himself, that he must work hard, that he must not waste the precious days or the gifts poured on him by nature—Ned Maxy would take that whisper with him until his own heart stopped too and he knew this.

The whisper of the paramedic country girl was there for him now too. He did not want to make too much out of it. Thousands must have been given this gift. He didn't want to be only another kind of fool, a sort of peeping Tom of charity.

But he *was* a new fool. Some big quiet thing had fallen down and locked into place, like a whisper of some weight. He had been granted contact with paradise. Something tired and battered and loud had just thrown in the towel. Ned Maxy could hardly believe the lack of noise. His awful '70s decade had gone past twenty years. Finally they were over.

The next day, Maxy in a daze got his rushed suit out of the cleaners and attended the wedding of the woman paramedic at a country church down between Water Valley and Coffeeville. He shook hands with the bride and groom, then stood out of the pounding heat under the shade of a tall brothering sycamore.

Nobody ever figured out quite who he was. Their faces were full of baffled felicity, as if each one was whispering: Well howdy, stranger, I guess.

Through Sunset into the Raccoon Night

You GET ON, AND ONE DAY IT OCCURS TO YOU YOU MIGHT BE doing something rather important for the last time. There is a bit of terror in this, but also an unexpected balm. Believe me, this thing can happen even when you still feel new as an eighteen-year-old.

Well she was long in the leg, well dressed, I mean a nice cut above what was called for in this small city. She was in her heels and silks even in the heart of July, waiting there in the bad air conditioning of her black Audi. I could see and feel her in her silk, with the sweat on her brow and her waist at panty-line, wearing her garter that said I WANT IT EVERY DAY. The city awaited her but she was waiting on me, hovering there against the curb in great patience. Because she said what I had was priceless. Her husband was a dumb mean doctor but she was splitting from him. Somehow I heard it that they had not touched each other in four years. Some interior decorator will charge in somebody's house and tell them things like this where we live, although since there's not a great deal to be gained hereabouts, the gossip tends to be more factual rather than vicious.

"So she's a pretty little thing," said Mary, a tiny woman, to me one day. But my woman was not little and off the point of pretty. "She's one of those who's been waiting too long for something, and doesn't know what it is now. She's a person who, I'll bet, says *no* a lot."

"You women are such experts on each other," I said.

"Yes, well, men pretend not to know things because they think it's manly. Raised in manly dumbness, even smart ones."

"You're just rude and hasty."

"You'd like to get your piece of her, *then* judge her. I know you. You've never looked at me the same since you had some of me."

"Nevertheless, she's something different."

"You mean a little difficult. Which really excites you."

"I like the way she calls me a real man, compared to her former mate, the surgeon. Very much. Yes."

"Oh boy, the double whammy. You get to go to bed with his fame and her body. You can't fool me. You like the way she *waits* on you, I mean lingers for you, around different places. That's important to you. *I* wouldn't, and now you've got a volunteer."

"No. You and I are just friends, big friends. Sometimes friends have to sleep together."

"Friends. I recall you were more ravenous than that."

"Ravished by loneliness at the time. That's what I remember. And I thank you."

"You were pathetic. Pretty good. But pathetic."

I have, like every man, seen all through my life lovely women waiting for someone somewhere. I always get involved, I mean in my head. These women, each wonderful, have elicited fine raptures and dreams. Waiting women, each postured in a special way, each in her separate nook of perfect waiting, a gallery that does not belong to me. They are prepared, sharpened, in their dresses and heels—or in their jeans and sandals, their brave halter tops—all open to the great psychological moment of some man's arrival. Negligence really is out of the question, with the right ones. And I have been that man over and over, besuiting myself for the expectant tastes of these lingering, watchful women. I imagine pleasing each one according to her most curious and valiant wants. The world for a few moments becomes wide and happy, not low and cramped. Even voluptuous. I bring extraordinary gifts to these patient women, thinking all day about them. So it is that I have made love to these women of my heady tableaux and been briefly a happier man for it. I hear the women speak softly, delighted by my presence. This is very good, since nobody else on the real earth truly needs me, not even the surgeon's wife Jane in the Audi out there as my business closes, soon. For the world I am impertinent and a malingerer.

I've never found anything I was good at worthy to do here. I surely don't blame the world for that. Through me runs an inveterate refractoriness, almost a will to lose. Really, a choice for the whining and pining, at ease in the infantry of unremarkable losers on the lower end of mobility. What I admire is anguish, casual faith, clothes, poise, and minor disaster, or the promise of it. I like the nose lifted a little. The pride of exemption, yet terror in solitude. This is a busy concept. Perhaps too busy.

"You drive her around as if she can't drive, in *her* car. What does this mean, exactly?" asked Mary, who always chuckled a little when she was being sincere.

"Because . . ." I don't know. "Because she is somewhat American YesterWorld, and I imagine it gives her the sense that fate now is out of her hands."

"But you simply go buy things together, little and big and far and near, like every other dull American couple, like old marrieds already."

This was true. And another thing was, there are a number of drugs in this country that, the way we are pitched, make you go buy things. Speed and broncho-dilators, Valium and booze, even Sudafed, make you want to gallop down and get some suddenly urgent thing. Marijuana, they say, is the king. Weed people hit one A.M. bargain barns like battle-field jackals. Zombies who buy have promoted me to the middle class just by accident. I have simply memorized a fair number of automobiles and have the parts ready for them almost by the time five words are out of their mouth. Yet I keep buying myself back down toward the lower class, as if with unconscious nostalgia. Towns you pass through around here often exist only to supply automobiles parts and service for people who have absolutely nowhere to go. The people keep hoisting me back up to the great bourgeoisie, over and over. I *can't* fail, my God, America! Show me some more oily jean cash, dirty pelt, warm lucre, young man! Put your hand in your pants and show me your dollars. Reach in your brassiere, O my sovereign nymphs and clayhill babush-kas. This may be work but I doubt it.

    And my word the wrecks the two of us see together in our hundred-mile radius. Wrecks and deaths for no reason at all. I'd guess three quarters of all wrecks are caused by people with no destination. They are caused by goons driving as with a heart attack in progress toward positively distinctly nowhere. Or fifteen miles at eighty per to get a couple Vidalia onions or a bowtie for some lowlife prom. I'm going on because those wrecks, wretched as the fact is, work as aphrodisiacs on both of us. Something about being alive next door to horror, then not and very hot. We stop and ask questions and then look at each other, shamed but blushing with need, a hard and troublesome thing for two who've yet to get in bed together. I've wondered if we owe now this strange duty to others in the future and must have our own pointless great wreck. From our jewel of a little city in south-ern Missouri, in this radius of want we get even through Memphis and down into northern Mississippi, where I saw a woman in an unknown rage drive repeatedly at high speed around the lot of a Sonic drive-in until she piled into a stone picnic table and killed herself.

I was almost sure I had witnessed the highest order of some kind of love, a love that put what the surgeon's wife and I had to shame. I refused to read any newspaper account of the incident and could not bear the sordid history that might be attached, because I saw, well, what I saw. Jane and I were so full of the wild gift of adrenaline once we looked at each other again, we could have ripped each other apart.

So were we *good* people then, because we did not follow through? No. Lovers are the most hideously selfish aberrations in any given territory. They are not nice, and careless to the degree of blind metal-hided rhinoceroses run amok. Multitudes of them cause wrecks and die in them. Ask the locals how sweet the wreckage of damned near everybody was around that little pube-rioting Juliet and her moon-whelp Romeo. Tornado in a razor factory, that's what sweetness. That poor woman with her neck broken over the steering wheel was in their league, don't tell me different. Without the stone picnic table, she'd have taken out all the help inside, and you'd have had the local scribes going for a year. Even the sad baritones on the box, too, tireless.

Once years ago I walked into a country juke saloon with a pistol to my head, but it was only a gag about music. Country folks don't *ever* get tired of the same song, they just want it maybe faster and deeper now and then. Or maybe it wasn't a gag. I'm just forty-two but sometimes very very weary.

I drive us, but I still do not have the main handle on whether we are in for construction or destruction. She has a way of looking at the floor and whispering *no*, unconsciously, eyes awfully flat and grim. Mary was absolutely right. I'm terribly glad she is my friend still. I'll hate to leave her behind, little prissy happy-bosomed gal from Joplin, the only near-beauty I've ever known who would hang around without liquor at a parts store.

As you can see, behind the counter of my casual anarchy at the store, where only I know where parts are, I've had time to think and come up with some high county epigrams of my own, because I have not found this life particularly pleasant and it's for damned sure my customers, the wheeled doofuses bred with a bad carburetor in their genes, aren't going to show me anything new. If I were greatly handsome or had promise I might kill myself, but I'm not giving wags the pleasure nor Mary the trouble. The wags have a bad enough time coping with internal combustion. What would they say about me anyway? I have no problems. I'm begging for minor disasters, like several wealthy people I've known. I couldn't cope with the options of wealth. The five or six I have in my present condition sometimes paralyze me. Also, the wealthy *like* money and are often so paranoid they pay someone to be after them, just so they will know distinctly who it is. To the man, every wealthy shop owner around the town circle here has a spread middle, a permanent bent neck toward the sidewalk from counting and playing with themselves, and nervous shoulders as if expecting to be poleaxed by a stranger from behind.

In my brief mournful summer in New York City years ago, I was attempting to get myself across as something I'm unwilling to discuss. All right, painting. Hustling my plain local stuff during the height of Warholism, inviting half smiles of almost Martian disdain from gallery owners, and with nobody else between me and them as I could guess they were begging there to be, since I was using precious seconds of their eyesight on my "work." I had at this time the almost mystic confidence of the autoanointed third-rater and must have sounded very much like Harry Truman.

I met a boy my age who had inherited vast wealth and seemed to like me. He had no job, did nothing but wander about, and I saw him exit one or two parties with his head down, looking run-over, with people gazing at his back. I had never met a true creep—a slug—although we used the item handily all through high school and college in Columbia (Missouri). But here was your real specie at last, a young man who could buy anything and had omitted to buy (possible, of course) a personality. He just hung around. I became his favorite and he would show up at bar dates uninvited, somehow finding out about my appointment with another person around Charles Street in the Village. He would appear, then stare at me, then at the floor; now with his face to me, turned again, after an unsettling hungry look. He wasn't gay as I suspected. He was nothing, just some sort of thing seeking my shade.

I had got to New York somehow without being conscious of Thomas Hart Benton, an artist from practically my own backyard—a real artist whose work, had I known it, would have discouraged me from New York entirely. But certain other artists loved the fact I'd never heard of him, and with them I was promoted in esteem. We were drinking a lot of cheap drinks in a cheap tavern and talking over my possibilities as a new savage (dream on), when this slug person, this creep, appeared again, looking at me, then down. I was drunk and angry over my treatment by the galleries, so I let him have it, very unlike myself. But he really was too much. I charged: What *do* you want? What are you after? Why are you here? Why aren't you *dead?* His narrow shoulders, the cocked-over head with chubby face—I can still see it—the small burned dirty eyes. I watched real pain and a faint smile come over him, such a hopeless and yet triumphant look as I'd never seen. He turned around, and after saying "I'm *so* sorry" with his back to me, he left and I didn't see him for a year.

I felt a hand on my shoulder. It was my artist pal, a boy from Maine not as drunk as I was. "You're the fourth one this summer. He stays and comes and interlopes and then an eruption from somebody like you he's been begging for, and he goes out whipped. I think he loves it, I know he does. He works you for abuse, gets it, and now he might be off stroking himself. Then he moves to another person."

I was staggered and instantly sober. My feel for the whole city was different now. I knew I was a loser too, but I was almost sick and very angry at what a fellow with every option like the creep could bring himself to. I thought I could even still smell his stale white oily body in here, like old margarine.

The rest of this story goes into the next summer when I was in the city just a week to flush out old mediocrities, and we were turning warm in mutual condolences, we less hopeful floggers, in the same tavern, when Elton, the creep, came in with the best-looking woman I had ever seen anywhere. He was unchanged, slumping, holding his mouth like a stunned halibut's, less than zero to say. Nobody had ever known where, under what cold bricks he lived. He was always just abruptly there, parachuted it seemed—that sudden—out of some ghastly greasy aerial pollution, face like the cunt of a possum. But the woman, why, she was with him and not vomiting, not vomiting at all. I think she was Brazilian. Pecan-skinned, silver-heeled, high-breasted all-out for summer. The despair in the tavern you could dip with a cup, and I wet my pants in sorrow and desire. That poor beauty, bought outright by Elton as his wife, was so reamed and gouged within one minute by every straight male eye in the bar she'd have been sausage under a few rags and heels had thought taken action. Elton—I did catch it, didn't I?—looked at me briefly and lifted one upper lip in what I think was an attempt at a smirk, although it was hard to tell with the dead eyes. All he did was stand there with her fifteen minutes. Neither one of them even had a drink. They said he was all sober now but he was such a creep nobody had ever known he was alcoholic, and if changed he looked worse now. Still, I believe I caught his smirk, which he did not have character enough to maintain. Then they strolled out, or she did, and he had his doughy oily palm on her crease, a whole other order of butt it was so good, and then I suffered the gnashing tragedy of never seeing her again, ever, in my life.

This I relay partially to explain I have not failed in only one place. No, I am cosmopolitan, tested. Also to assure you as in those fat bright books you might read that the truly wealthy are often true worms. But not so much this as to warn myself about the surgeon's wife, especially waiting right now in the Audi for her special abuse, maybe, a different sort than Elton's, but I've an edge of sickness about this too. Something in her leans over on me out of her soul, a quality of boiled spaghetti. She appears and sits and waits a bit *too* much. She has told me that her first child (she has another) was created by her hand from the condom of her husband, herself alone in the bathroom while he slept, in the slyness of determined motherhood. He did not want children now, in school. Why'd she tell me? Does she see it as adorable or valiant? Is it a testimony of slightly appalling urges in the womb or an ugly little act of deceit and control? I can't tell, honestly. She appears and sits and waits a bit *too* much. There is, without my having possessed her yet, a bit too much preparation and dullish watchful stare about her, and a persistent slackening in her jaws, though she has a red marvelous mouth, as if she were sucking at me in bits and might become at her climacteric *all* mouth and vacuum, oral entirely, have me down the maw with only my poor shoes sticking out. I fear in short that *she* is a creep. But that's not even the worst fear. As with Elton I know now I was frightened he wanted near me because *I* was a creep. Creeps go for creeps and the veterans know who they are instantly. Because a loser like me can have honor—as the used have honor and life even in their outrage, while the user has mere habit—and the creep none. Was evil ever this low, banal, and gaudy? Imagine Elton, who was indeed the picture of Mr. Trump without money, but more slumped and even oilier, but the same mouth and dead eyes. And Elton went directly to *me*. I knew the others he went to: they were at least latent creeps, without exception—the common denominator my friend from Maine left out.

I won't tell Mary everything, but it's necessary I listen to her, because I'm beginning to feel threatened, without consummation, only long preparation by our *words,* our merchandise, and our car wrecks. A certain song had come out I'd heard on the FM, and now I owned it. By Radiohead. The name of it exactly: "Creep." It is a haunting thing, sung by a creep to a goddess oblivious to him. I think of Elton. "What am I doing *here?*" the creep pleads, and it hits me very deeply, a pain of perfect acknowledgment. Why do I like it so much? Why has Mary asked me to please quit playing it over and over, paying no attention to the other songs on the CD? What am I so *tranced* about? she demands. Why don't you go out and just rake her down, the doctor's ex-fox? Not all women are good. Some women have *tragic* pussies, she pushed on to get to my head. I'd never heard Mary use a bad word and I stopped the music.

"There's something wrong with women who talk and wait and plan too much. My friend. Why *you?* There are certainly others more in her league. Why is she still in *town,* even?" she says.

Now I'm truly scared in my concupiscence, my ready loins, my thighs with some muscle definition all sightly from private squats with seventy pounds on my shoulders, my calves corded and well-tennised—these secret extraordinary gifts all for her waiting. But I frown at good Mary. Then comes the patient smile and the hooded eyes, taught by example by my own father in home combat. "I wish I was special! But I'm a creep!" the defeated tenor of Radiohead howls. "I don't belong here!"

God what freedom in that statement. I just adore it and am terrified too.

Elton, at last confessed, at last! Elton! Forgive my abuse, little rich man!

Besides buying various rugs, mats, futons, pillows, and even sleeping bags for us to have our earnest postures on in different rooms together, Jane is planning her own home for the first time in her life, she says. Her dearly own. It will be a tour. I sense I am something of an agent of travel for her. The home is going up north of the city, near a lake, on a hill with big trees and hanging moss around it. She stands spread-legged like Marilyn over that grate in New York in the empty boarded air of her rooms, while I watch her high eloquent rump and tennis legs, just a slight burn of tan on them, and fine ankles into slung-back short heels. With her back to me I can almost bring back the Brazilian, Elton's bride. She intends to be "courted" this time. She wants stages. She loves it that we met on the tennis courts, like college children. I'd been so long without a woman, I could wait and get excited only in the head for a while, as you can get unhungry by not eating long enough. I think I had not, until Jane, ever had dessert at a restaurant and stared slyly for two hours at every twitch of a woman's eyebrows, blue in the groin. I go to bed alone. No, really, it is not disagreeable. My head language becomes cleaner, my instincts have a sudden balm, and I feel right tidy in this love, if that's what I have.

A nun once told me she had been constantly in love all her life, a sweet mental love more superb and wider than any touching could supply.

"Impossible," I said.

"Well damn you," she added, "Mister."

She too must have guessed I was a creep, because her voice had run out scarily as from another person sitting beside her on the airplane. And *she* was shocked. I was shot with cold.

I have lately thought about my birthplace, St. Louis, and what is wrong there. Eminent creeps have issued from there as by some necessity of the environment. T. S. Eliot and William Burroughs, maybe they are profound, but does anybody miss the sluggish dead-staring creep quality in them either? Jane is also from there. I could never quite decide about the hipster of my New York summer, the paragon, Miles Davis, who in his autobiography gave us the nice term *country hip* for bluesmen along the river. But sometimes there was a rancid flatness to him, even beyond his heroin glare. The surgeon's wife—I call her that when I put her away a bit to study—loves the right clothes, I love the right clothes, and Miles Davis held them near sacred. I want to be country hip like Davis's friends, smooth as a modest flower behind the counter of the parts store. Jane seems more *born* in the latest shift, her hair fluffed casually by some fag offstage, impeccable.

She told me one afternoon the only other man she had loved since her husband was a man dying of cancer whose intensity in life and lovemaking was so beautiful it made her cry, and she knew I'd do that for her too. I could almost feel myself at that moment writhing in her arms like a dolphin on dry land.

I worry that I've buried and denied the fact there were so few truly admirable adults during my upbringing in St. Louis. Were they there and I was such a creep I missed them all? Did they all become just a little less vicious as they aged, more reconciled and easy, simply because they had no more teeth and were horrified that they'd be ignored and scorned? These men and women became softer and kinder, with infinite patience too, especially with their grandchildren. But I did not trust them. It has been said about a successful painting acquaintance of mine—by quick Mary—an only child rather clubby in his friendships with "real" men like hunters and other painters of the hard-angled quotidian, that once he had got all he could out of unkindness, he turned to kindness. Then I regard the spacial grace of Indian tennis players. Places *do* make people. There was a family in St. Louis I lived with, sleeping with their divorced mother. Only her son, the more Southern one for some reason, with his easy strength, his quiet voice, his hesitation to judge, was bearable. The daughter, every day on the backseat of the car as she was taken to school, said, demanding: "Turn on the radio, please." The *please* just an irony in her mouth, in a flat, mean voice. The mother obliged as if hypnotized, never pausing to find that rock-and-roll button for the brat. One day I couldn't bear it any longer, but when she was out of the car to school I did not attack. Rather I started weeping because of the sadness of being around this hugely indulged vixen, and I knew love would die soon because I couldn't stand the home life that made her possible.

The long study that idiots give themselves, the endless excuses of the weak and vicious. The willingness to go public with hideous disease as if that were the primary goal in life. Why else am *I* writing? Two men were playing beside me on the next tennis court last spring. They were, as they *hit the ball*, yelling to each other about their exercises, their protein intake, their reps, their lats, their pecs, their squats. Screaming their charts at one another. Later on one of them smiled at me in a café as if we were close buddies, since I had been there to listen, nothing amiss here, hands out my kindred. I had a hard time frowning him off, this monster. His body looked to me like something foul and bought, a meat suit.

Now the house is done, Thanksgiving has passed, and I have had Jane in all her rooms with the ardor of long dreamers, and the wait proves all worth it, an instance where the flesh has really gone into more pleasures than even the dreams. But I knew she was wonderful, and that begging for minor disaster seemed artificial, like something I had cultivated from a book by a French existentialist in college, just in order to seem properly grave.

Not especially Sartre or Camus, but much of college now anyway seems like an endless qualification and rebuke to pleasure by the same kind of middle-aged people I grew up with, so that the bean of the reasonable and moderate would grow to the size of a tree in the head you could barely see out of by the time you became an adult yourself, thus to sit in your room and review the world, choked by moderation in all things. I did not see happy middle-aged men until I began going to roadhouses to hear and *watch,* more, rhythm-and-blues musicians, some of them with white hair and bellies, having a fine time on what must have been sub-minimum wages. I hold no brief for the universal holiness of African-Americans that goes down as commandment in much of the press today. But I was overwhelmed by the sight of dark older Americans having fun. Most, I loved them for their bellies. They'd been having it a long time, on much good collards, fatback, and cheap whiskey.

Jane was five years older than me. I'm not sure whether we were jaded eccentrics or new discoverers of the body electric. In different rooms decorated in subtle "rhythm and hue" changes—some help from the St. Louis granny of an interior decorator she had in the wings, a naughty queer I liked too—I delivered myself unto Jane, at her shy sugges-tions, as French, Greek/African (where the bottoms are of more interest), Italian, then just straight-on Missouri mis-sionary, always talking while making love the way she said her ex, no real man, never did. Jane had a girl's voice I found highly arousing, and I hope I did not sound too silly like Harry Truman as a mad poet, because Jane could sing, I mean around the house she sang anything well, on key and with luxury. I asked her one day, laughing, why we didn't sometimes just get on an airplane and visit some of the coun-tries, since I was so busy enacting the United Nations. I'd be glad to pay for it all. Then she shocked me, and I began looking down at the lake below her house, a beautiful but saddening view through the hanging moss.

"I never traveled. I never intend to travel. I don't like far parts. We traveled enough getting our things for this house. We've got the big-screen TV and all the good sta-tions. What more is there to see?"

She'd got a handsome divorce settlement and had her own money anyway, and a doctor father who'd given her this place as a gift. This luck of mine, well I quit boasting inside about it just then. The garter I gave her with I WANT IT EVERY DAY printed on, which she had worn until we got married—I asked her about it. She said wearing it nude with hose on had always made her feel foolish. Now I felt like a pressing creep without much to give from my world.

In my world I had straightened and ordered my supplies and parts in the showroom and taken down the posters of half-naked girls leaning across the hoods of Maseratis and Lotuses, things that pleased me and made my customers buy something expensive for the sheer hell of it, a ticket to half-brassieres in foreign towns. Mary helped me. In our days of intimacy she'd never said anything about the poster women, and now made no fun of me when they came down at Jane's request.

Mary and I could never have made it as lovers. I don't like to sleep with women who are smarter than me. But I'd never had a real friendship with a woman until Mary, and I was enjoying the pleasant wonder of it very much, when I was not suicidal. Now the rare times Jane came in the store, if Mary was there Jane looked through her with such frozen smiling malice that Mary offered to never come around again. She had plenty to do, with her own painting, which she could have sold even more of at good fees if she'd cared. But I begged her not to leave. I don't believe I could have stood it.

On Jane's idea of having the world on our big-screen television: The very next day I had some trouble with the boy who works my stockroom. I knew he was on something, but he didn't steal and he did a fair job. I was amused by his old-man's miseries at age twenty-three, compounded by the fact he couldn't read and thought I didn't know that. That afternoon he came in bleary and in a rage and asked me if I kept a pistol. He needed to kill somebody who had just insulted him for the last time.

"Why no, Byron. My God, fool. You'll go to prison. Think this out."

"I have. They got color TV in prison."

He was high on something, but he had never been more serious. He was ready for his life to be over and resign himself, with relish, to the high-gloss realm of somebody else's vision from now on. I could barely reply. I'd never known how he hated himself and his life so much. Even in my worst depressions I was still snob enough to know I would take out myself in my own act, in my own show, never by the congealed vision of others who need you half-dead in a chair to own the world. Then I asked Jane something that had bothered me and I was afraid to know.

"You said I was priceless. That I had something priceless. But what is it? Why am I special?" The fear was creeping. I was hard bothered all over again.

She thought too long, as if it weren't really that big a question and she'd forgotten.

"Well . . . I saw that painting of yours you didn't want me to see, under your bed in your townhouse apartment, about a year ago. I really like it. It's very great art. I loved you even more for thinking it was no good. Your very high standards, all private like that."

But it was wretched and derivative and never got much past simple meanness, like much of my work. The only reason it had any merit was I'd done a fair cartoon in the Thomas Hart Benton mode showing ghouls—my customers—with long arms and grief-stricken faces pulling out automobile parts from their bodies—you saw the outlines where they'd been ripped out, bloody—and demanding replacements. All of this with a hideous backdrop, too yellow. I kept it as a reminder, sleeping over it, that it was as far as I would ever push in creation. It was only a milestone. I had no vanity about it.

"You made those people out the real Frankensteins they are, like those people around those wrecks we saw. Thank God we're not like them at all, what a world. You cutey."

"But *we* were there. They made us hot, Jane, remember?"

"I got hot loving that I wasn't them. It still gets me hot knowing you're not my ex-husband. He was so dumb and dull. Never once did he say my cunnie was the best in the world, like you do. I'm so so really happy you're not him, baby. He was good, he was successful," she began tearing up, and I was amazed, "but let me tell you this: he never had high standards. He accepted just about anything the way it was and just had these tired grunts every now and then."

It's impossible to overdeclare my disdain for dying a wise old man, knowing every salient point, sitting there in my last room as with a multistory library in a cone over my ears. I was hugely sorry I'd asked about my pricelessness, having learned only what I was not. That our love was going along so well out of spite, like how many other loves?— the same, no different. "Living well is the best revenge." "Prepare to make the memories," say the beer and camera ads. All you need is beer, camera, and revenge and you're a player.

I walked out of the house down the hill toward the lake. I needed to talk to Mary, but then I found a gift by accident. I was sitting on the dam getting bit by chiggers and mosquitoes and deer flies but refusing to move or get in the water, which I needed to do.

An animal came up next to me, which I believed to be an apparition in my periphery. It was about the size of a big house cat. It kept moving slowly towards me the two hours, it must have been. But I looked ahead, not even a weed in my mouth, nothing in front but a blind thousand yards. I finally felt it so close that I looked around. It was a large and handsome raccoon, regarding me and not moving now as I stared straight at it. Its hair was so deep and rich, brown and black, it seemed beyond real, so prosperous out here on the beaches of the encroaching shore lots with their moody houses on the hill. I stood, and after retreating only inches to gather itself back, it took stock of me without nervousness then eased up closer and closer—a yard away—and decided I was no threat. It was without the ordinary panic of these careful beasts. Did it know me? Was I something like a body washed up out of a deep lake, the odor of a sunburned slug? He looked to be truly working me for a few minutes. I got uncomfortable and started walking around the lake. This lover of marine carrion fell in step just a little to my right on the water side.

Lovers, even middle-aged lovers I guess, may not be good people, but if they were like me just now, after the physical ardor of two months after a wait of over a year, they do have innocence. They're so worn out there is hardly anything left but the sleepy wonder of infants. I was stumbling along as if on the ground of the moon, reading everything with intense color in a doubled hurtful light, near the result of those drugs I took just a few of at Columbia, but with more suspense because I was clean. The raccoon paced along. When I knew it did not want to eat me, I think we became chums. We walked around the lake and back to where I was, and this thing we repeated three or four times a week in the last of the winter, which was mild.

Everybody knows raccoons are graceful. I regard them as so refined in beauty they are almost like a work of art let out to eat, especially this big sleek friend who wouldn't seem to mind going back and watching television with me when Jane was out of the house. I felt better, going around the shore, sometimes watching the animal freeze, poke, and snatch when it wanted something tasty out of the water.

The élan of the Indian tennis players occurred to me as I looked forward to the European tournaments on the big-screen Toshiba. I hoped there were some Indian tennis players left to watch, with their sweet moves, their gentlemanship, a power beyond victory and defeat to me, much in rebuke to our wearisome national jocks and deranged narcissists like McEnroe. I didn't give the raccoon a name even as he became nearly a walking roommate. You should not name something more elegant than you, I thought. I didn't even know its sex. Maybe it was a newly mated older boy like me taking a couple hours off from the little woman back at the castle.

I was near broke again, with all my buying for the house, back to the lower class. I'd never taken money from Jane and didn't intend to. Our house felt like a rented thing to me, with none of my purchased future in it. I'd built a muscadine arbor one morning out of heavy stakes with lattice board for a roof. We would see it from our rear bay window on the slope into the lake. It was my first yard idea ever. I wanted a grape bower with a love couch underneath— somehow an all-weather one, if they made them. I wanted the raccoon to visit and eat the grapes, maybe even bring his family over. I expected the thing, in fact, to one day give up his beastly quietness and begin chatting with me. Or I would become a whole new animal, enough to chat in *its* language. Jane and I could ravish each other on the couch even into old age. I was sad, but so what? This was my only marriage and I didn't intend to retreat from it. Maybe I was copying the decorator, the old granny with his erotic room ideas, or competing with him. I was proud.

But when Jane looked down in the yard at it she didn't show delight. I could sense there was something wrong with it now. It wasn't on television.

Then I got back from a trip to Kansas City one afternoon. Jane embraced me at the door, all bright, and said she had a surprise for us. I spied down toward my old arbor construct. It had been torn down and replaced by one in green metal exactly the shade of the trees. The granny had told her where she could get one, the whole outfit, and his men had put it up for her. I went almost insane. It was our first large fight—nearly all one-sided by me—but I felt eternity in it. I almost struck her, there with her eyes seeming dead and glib to me all of a sudden. I told her the raccoon wouldn't likely come near that thing.

"The raccoon? The *what* raccoon?!"

"*My* raccoon. For the grapes."

"What, have you invited him? What's this raccoon? You're sick!"

She slammed away to her retreat in the plump covers of our king-size bedroom where more Japanese television was.

Yes, I was sick, and it continued. I was not the same, maybe am still not. I've got myself in trouble, a minor disaster I rather like—not a well man. I neglected my raccoon friend and imagined that it cared.

In the early spring I began playing more tennis, but not with Jane, who cared less now for the game. I played with little Mary. Not in spite, either. There was no special reason to tell Jane, and Mary's now careful friendship was too precious to lose.

One day I went down to the courts with too much beer in me. I knew I could not drink over two beers without going straight into depression, more a desert than an abyss for me, longer and no abrupt way out with great effort. See here, I have sought help professional and amateur for myself. I've tried to heal myself, always a bit sick that the cluttered mentocracy of self-study that afflicts this fat nation had enrolled me too. I agreed with the last food doctor entirely on the beer and had been much better for it. I'd never been a real drinker anyway, just a medicator of joylessness.

Mary keeps running and trying, dear heart, even without a great deal of strength, but with the advantage of growing up on a family court in Memphis with a mother who was a tour player. I'm just a bit better, without a single formal lesson. I watch a good player—the Indians—and try to absorb their spirit. There is a dullish way of playing perfect tennis, by all the percentages, that causes tennis burnout to the young even in their twenties—the young of a certain sensitivity. They get tired of the geometry and the predictions, their coaches and families. I've been close to that just by the repetition of a few weeks of near-perfect play. Maybe I'd drunk the beer to make the match more even between Mary and me. She was winning and I was not slacking.

One of those body men of the same pair—who played beside me ranting about their exercise and food regimen months ago—came over as I was beginning to serve.

"Say, did you know you were always late with your backhand, just a little late? You should step up to the ball more, get to the height of its arc, and be in front of it."

Hardly without a pause, I dropped my racket and slapped him in the face. I'd never hit a man with a full fist, and in this case the result would have been even sillier if I had. He popped me so fast with the ham of his forearms, twice, I was out cold for a time. I woke up sitting, with his face over me and into mine, now with more concern than anger. He was smiling. Then he must have smelled the beer on me. Mary was up by me, amazed on her little legs.

"You shouldn't come out here drinking, pal. I'm sorry, but you're very lucky I'm a belt. I only told you you were late with your backhand," the man said.

"I've been late with my backhand for thirty years. It's the way I play, it's fun that way. You fucking loudmouth pig."

Mary moved down to get between him and me as he took a step, saying *no* to both of us. He wore athletic sports glasses. In his horror over my infirmity, he cut into me with a high-beamed glass stare that reminded me of every imperious monster of life that had ever hounded me. I almost fainted with hatred, overcome by all my failures at once, and proud of them too.

Afterwards Mary and I drank even more beer in my closed store together. I took out a new Jaguar poster with an even nuder woman poised in a diaper on the hood, her toes stretched out as just then in the moment of sexual crisis. I tacked her up. She was more Ford than Jaguar.

"Yes, and I think I'm separating from Jane. This antiseptic thing is coming on too strong. We're going to just be a laboratory with the right wallpaper soon. She even asked me if I thought we'd still make love after age fifty. My God, fifty. That's probably gotten dirty too. Or unkempt. That's what it is about those St. Louis Midwestern people. Their fear of soil, wood, anything that could leave a stain—*that's* why they're creeps. Want to pave the world, they're paving the goddamn beaches, they want designer *nursing homes* for resorts." And so on. "She doesn't even like sex, I'll bet. She just wants a picture of it."

I thought I'd get some agreement from Mary. But now she scolded me, and I quit the beer.

"You're not separating. No you are not. Separating is all you've done since I've known you. And you will work with Jane, you will compromise. At your age it's just indecent, you, to always *want* to be a social nigger. You won't get along without her. You'll get worse."

"We might strike up something again, you and me," I said.

"Not a prayer. You're *had.* You worked for it hard to be had, and you're not stepping out now! You're married, Royce! You're so absolutist. You think heaven's supposed to *feel* like heaven. If you quit this, I know this: you'll get old and tired instantly, with all your little principles intact. Just old and tired."

Now she was wet in her eyes.

But my raccoon, *my* arbor, my self! "A house should be a boat on this planet, riding nature. She wants a high-profile mausoleum, a monolith with a lawn like a pool table around it." This felt original to me, and I was in rare beer eloquence, with my face good and bruised by that fiend on the court. I felt good and brave.

Mary simply left, on her little legs, and I had the shop alone.

So now our love life is getting worse, although the raccoon came right up for the muscadines when they were out two years later. It didn't care if the poles were green metal. I fixed a couch under the vines that Jane seemed to like, but easing her toward long talks—we had nothing left to say—and pleasures under the moon will be a job. Sometimes on the television we'll see a number of people, peasants, driven off into a chasm in the desert by charioteers with great-looking helmets in pursuit, and she'll get a little warm. Sometimes there's a sort of new kindness about her. I saw her feeding the raccoon with a can of premium King Oscar sardines once, out there by herself with it. I don't think she knew I could see through the vines from the house.

She got bored and the granny decorator, with his delicious whip of a tongue, wanted her to work with him, since she was educated to his home touches. I imagine he's seen with her at very good restaurants where they eat in St. Louis. She eats with him a lot more than with me, and that's fine, really, since we can't talk very much. One week there was a sort of scandal, rather pathetic, when the old granny was lying in his own bed playing with himself in easy view of several straight young workmen busy at his house. Jane took his side. I was surprised how this desperation endeared him to me too, sad fellow. Because I'm on his team. The coach has sent me in whether I wanted to play the last losing quarter or not. I look at my lean face in the mirror and see less a younger man than a thing in progress to a remarkable death's head.

Thanks deeply for listening as I wind down this scratchy log. I've gone back to the Presbyterian church of my youth a few times, alone and secretly. White church music is still awful and middle-aged everybody still appalls me, especially the sudden careful holiness they're given over to, having bought a ticket to a proverb convention—I judge.

Yet the very few graceful, profound, and bewildering words of Our Saviour do get through to me more and more, so different from this loser's, lost like a two-headed snake in jabber at itself, condemned to my own story like somebody already in an Italian hell. I am slow, I am windy. I have so little vision, engaged in this discourtesy of length and interminable excuse, but seeing bits of light here and there ahead. The Indian tennis players aren't winning much anymore, but I hope they're still around.

Tell me. Did Our Saviour die *because* he was right, or is it that he simply was right and then he died? Tell me, let's chat. I'll be mostly in the shop.

The Agony of
T. Bandini

TIGER BANDINI WAS A SHORT SORT OF PROWLING FELLOW WITH plump red lips and black ashy cheeks. He came from sports people but even to other hard-bitten fans he was over the line. He knew intimately about all the quick and larger hitters in American football. Above all he liked the linebackers and other violent crushers. He worshiped the violent crush. His eyes would close as if in a dream when he talked about Lawrence Taylor, for instance. He would begin screaming and white liquid would form at the corners of his lips. Giants fans in the bars who had begun in agreement with him would edge away and huddle together to avoid him. But Bandini was in a zone of screaming delight and was not conscious of this. One day after a Giants game on the television he went into a tirade of celebration and lost consciousness. They let him lie there on the floor, and in a few minutes he was back up on the bar, his eyes gone to slits and a vicious grin wrapped around another whiskey. He was whispering, "Taylor. Taylor." He had been there since morning and when he left he got in his car and killed another man in a bad head-on accident.

He was forbidden a driver's license in perpetuity by the judge. His family had struggled in measures grievous to them to keep Bandini out of prison and Bandini advised himself that he could no longer exist in his own town in upper New York state under the burden of shame and guilt.

Before his college experience was interrupted by the accident Bandini had met a pair of Southern boys who were crazed for the work of William Faulkner, and even more

127

crazed as their homesickness grew. They could quote long passages from Faulkner that sounded to Bandini like a black preacher schooled on an enormous dictionary. Bandini sided with blacks, especially now that he was in disgrace and felt shunned. The Southern boys, like Faulkner, had elaborate reasons for doing almost anything. Bandini was impressed by this. He felt he was in the world of pain and ruin now after the wreck, but he saw there were elaborate reasons for it, and he relished this, as he drank only beer now at the end of the bar, only sometimes shouting. Ruin talked to him.

For instance, their college was not a very good college and was even falling apart physically. The buildings were erected by inferior contractors supported by the New York Mafia. Around the campus, interior and exterior walls fell down in chalky gravel that the students walked over daily. Sections of ceiling were apt to drop out, especially after a big snow or rain. Bandini liked to expatiate on the complexities of this in a patient beered-up review of the history of the New York Mafia. The Southern boys agreed nothing worthy was as plain as it seemed. The only worthy subjects were coiled up and crossed like nylon fishing line. Like them, Bandini began to speak much of destiny and twists of fate. This comforted him. Much was inevitable and bound to the blind dice-thrower fate. Fishing line left overnight would coil of its own.

So he thought it was in the dice and natural that he wind up way down south in a rental home in the precincts of the great author Faulkner himself. The town was storied and cozy, filled with shady lanes under great oaks. Around even his poor house in the student section was a bank of weeping willows.

One night, uncommonly drunk on Jägermeister, Bandini fell into them. It was midmorning when he awoke in a dream of green wigwam. A skinny cat came in there with him. Bandini took off all his stinking clothes, picked up the cat, and began weeping. This seemed a sad and wonderful place in here. He cursed the pavement and steel outside and did not come out of the trees until evening, when the cat began mewing loudly. The animal continued mewing in the house but he had got too drunk all over again on a pint of sloe gin thrown out of a car into the willows and did not understand what it wanted since he hardly ever ate himself. He looked at the creature and passed out on his nasty fluorescent sofa.

In the night he woke up the cat was still calling out and he recognized what it wanted because now he was hungry too. He put the cat in his overcoat pocket and walked a mile and a half to Kroger's intending to provide a feast for the both of them and pushing the cat down by the shoulders. It scratched and hurt Bandini's hand gravely but he staggered on. His cheeks were blown and red, and were like somebody had thrown a full ashtray on them.

Bandini had forgot his wallet, and he was far, far from his resources, a cold desert away it seemed. So in the lonesome store with scant personnel he put his free hand down into the aquarium and shoplifted two great lobsters and set them in the other pocket. Now he was truly fastened in by the hands on both sides and he went out the front electric door with a rictus of his big red mouth and some kind of song it might have seemed to the policeman, bored in a car. He got far out in the lot before he could truly whimper. The night manager came out and the policeman swung toward Bandini in his vehicle but Bandini saw this and scampered like a goat-fiend over the hill behind a branch bank and into the thorns, dead wortvine, and minor gullies where only the most wretched of animals went, and down closer to another road he stumbled on yet another bottle with half its liquor, so he secured the lobsters and drank, then he stayed to the backyards and overcame the trifling fences of the middle-aged and wifeworn, where had they shined a light on him they would have seen a man near vomitous with joy.

Tiger Bandini had got new lungs and legs off the boon of drink and he was again that twisting shifty dodger who had almost made the team nine years ago in the town close to the Canadian line. He came out of an alley into the town square free of the police, crafty and game, rid of the pain in his hands, which failed against the found whiskey. He tossed the bottle into a grate and saw in the cold moon before him the courthouse statue of the lone Confederate looking curiously southward. He became infatuated right off and with great conviction he emancipated the cat and lobsters, then began climbing the ten feet of pedestal and statue. He did not see the cat remain in the gutter only a short time before it ran at both lobsters huddled and alien there.

Bandini had a free wide heart for the vanquished. He scaled toward the man, all fours engaged, in an act of hunching and embracing. The policeman had driven up to witness this remarkable love, as Bandini almost reached the boots of the defeated. The policeman heard the man cry out like a thing impaled and then it was too ugly for him to watch anymore. The odor of rank sea and a low hissing brought the officer to kneel with his light. Above him, Bandini was going nowhere.

In jail Bandini was given the drunk tank where Cruthers, a lean black man, squatted. Cruthers was a police informer and chauffeur for a town writer who specialized in the burden of history.

Cruthers had twelve or fourteen DUIs. He claimed to be a sergeant in the Vietnam conflict who carried about an M-60, his sweet big baby, and mowed down hundreds. He slept in a tree and went native, a lizard of death from above, abandoned to independent slaughter by an army who did not love it enough and did not have the hair.

Cruthers would drive the writer to far parts, even New York, where the writer would introduce him to his cronies as the burden of history. Late at night with enough whiskey the writer and Cruthers would listen to Sinatra and Presley on a small cassette player and began weeping over the Vietnam dead and the Confederate dead, and, appropriate to the writer's novel, the Korean dead. When Sinatra sang, it was the dead of World War II.

The lobsters and cat and scaling of the soldier were precious to the writer and Bandini was in solid at the writer's campus bungalow. He read up on Bruce Catton and could account for the Northern agony, better and better, when the topic moved over to Those Who Fell once Elvis sang his medley of "Dixie" and "Battle Hymn of the Republic" with the highly sincere Las Vegas band behind him.

Bandini insisted Cruthers move in with him and share his lot and the few hundred a month he got from his parents to stay out of New York. In fact he rather kidnapped Cruthers from the writer. But this was all right, since the writer was growing tired of Cruthers a little. Lately he had begun running the car out of gas and leaving it in mean places where crack fiends prowled and respected nothing. Also there was the problem of Cruthers always being in jail to be bailed out. Some money had disappeared too.

Bandini filled up the old shabby yellow house with history books. He was studying to be a student in the future, but this could wait. Through the writer he was let in to practice sessions of the football team, and he watched from the sidelines for hours, memorizing the players, especially the swift monstrous crushers. The coaches did not know what to make of the screaming little man with the New York accent who seemed to know and hate the weaknesses of individual players even more than they did. He used the word *pussy* a great deal. Soon he was asked to quiet down or leave. But he seemed to think of himself as a man with true work and vicious responsibility. Bandini knew that college players were semipro recruits only tenuously connected to the university. Half of them were not on familiar terms with the phrase *alma mater*. Bandini loved this. He wanted to think of the boys as pure cruising crushing meat, a kind of express ham. He was partial as always to the blacks, who he thought of as bursting out of their little nasty nowheres into the howling arenas of the world in the manner of Spartacus. This was their only shot and Bandini worshiped this wild simplicity.

The first time I saw Bandini in public trouble was after a game our team had lost in November when it was first turning chilly. Twilight was coming on and we filed out under the end zone stands. In the end zone we had a sort of rowdy club made up of professors and artists. It was fun seeing the touchdowns and murderous defensive plays from just a few feet away. Bandini sat with us and always brought Cruthers to the games with him. Without cease he would yell insults at the players, naming them, when he saw an error. He became hoarse doing this but never relented even when the game was far gone and the loyal were trickling out.

Under the stands a large professor who was also drunk had not cared for Bandini's style and was beating Bandini on his head, really pounding him, as the man's wife and Cruthers looked on. But Bandini would rise and rise again, crying out hoarsely. The wife seemed angrier than the man beating Bandini, actually. She had been personally insulted but the large professor was going about clobbering Bandini in a dutiful way, just socking him as if stamping the price on groceries. Cruthers was holding the man's coat and smiling. Bandini would not fall and stay, and when he rose once, I heard his hoarse voice still going, hoarse in a whisper through his big bloody lips. He was still yelling about the game, the errors. He was barely acknowledging the professor, and I believe there was even a little smile on Bandini's lips, a tolerant thing, as if this were a small social misunderstanding.

Months later, toward the end of my own serious drinking life, I was in a bar in an alley off the center of town. This bar prided itself on its roughneck and biker atmosphere in a town devoted to campus fashion in nearly everything. A crowd made way on the dance floor in front of the rockabilly band. I thought at first it was Bandini dancing by himself. But he was doing his moves and staggering from having been hit. A man in a leatheroid long cowboy coat had struck him for defending Cruthers, who had been dancing with a white girl. Cruthers was still standing beside the girl with his arm around her shoulders sweated up from the dance. I noticed he was beholding it all with an expression of implacable scorn.

I really felt for Bandini, who went over to a booth by himself and sat there a long time, with an awful bruise rising on the side of his face. He was saying something over and over to the table but you couldn't hear it for the band. I asked him if he was all right.

He lifted up his head and said: "I'm always all right."

I heard that later in the night, however, Bandini had come out of the booth having shed his clothes. He had begun dancing and whirling. The boy who told me this commented that Bandini had an enormous penis, a thing almost not a part of him, it seemed. Nobody could believe it, and the band quit. Bandini lifted his penis and shook it all around at every-body, baiting each and every one, as it was quiet now.

"You can't hurt me. Nothing you can do. You can't hurt me."

They were astounded but nobody seemed to mind that much. Bandini was in bad luck, however. There were two cops at the door and they broke through and hauled off Tiger Bandini, who still proclaimed himself hurt-proof. One drunk woman dancer began crying and saying what an awful thing that was, that it was too much like Jesus and it was a terrible, terrible thing to witness. She was hysterical.

I visited Bandini and Cruthers several times that year. I was running out of friends to drink with and it seemed that my worst anguish over a drink came on Sunday evenings when all the liquor was gone and the stores were shut. I think Bandini and Cruthers were moderating their drinking some-what now after the incident at the bar. Cruthers I'd guess was simply a vast consumer and not strictly alcoholic. He simply drank whenever it was provided and you never saw him begging for a beer. He was a seasoned blithe leech and the campus provided him with a perennial supply of white liberal donors. He had a certain style and I never saw him thank anybody for a drink they had bought him. Bandini always seemed to have a few cold beers or the good part of a bottle left on Sunday nights.

The last night I visited he had two whole bottles and half a case of Heineken. It was his birthday and they had had a party yesterday, he said.

After three drinks I could not get a lift, only the poi-soned flat feeling. I told Bandini I thought I was alcoholic. This made him very angry, not at me but at the idea.

"You are *not!*" he insisted. "Don't take the cheap way out. Nobody is really . . . anything. Everybody is just a collision."

I wondered where he had got that. Around the room, all over the sofa and the bed, were books of history. I noticed markers were in all of them just a few pages deep. He seemed to be reading many at once instead of one at a time.

I was over there hours talking history, football, and great art. I started talking about women but that stopped everything for a while. There was a long pause during which I drank very rapidly and finally felt a little. Bandini had nothing to say about women. He looked at me vacantly. Cruthers said he liked sleeping with a fat woman when it came winter. He said he had children about who were pretty. Bandini was flat to this too.

I recalled then I had never seen Bandini with a woman. He was not gay, but I had never even seen him in conversation with a woman.

But he was getting emotional now, well into the good whiskey along with Cruthers, who seemed to be getting sadder.

Bandini put a tape of the soundtrack to the movie *Platoon* in a small player and a trumpet began crying out.

The two of them were moving into something and I'll never forget it. Cruthers leaned against the window, and outside, the cat that Bandini had saved sat poised like a monitor on the other side of the screen with an orange moon behind it. They listened intently to the soundtrack and I felt to say anything would be like speaking aloud in church. Cruthers got to shuffling and became moodier and distant. Bandini raised his head and said to Cruthers softly, "Tell it all."

The mood had gotten almost holy and eerie.

Cruthers began talking.

"I could sleep and make myself little but I always woke up the second anything anybody in range. I could smell them, my nose wake me up. I was on that tree crotch and had me a good limb with my honey and I start fucking her. They come over a hill five black pajamas in a row across like they was hunting rabbits. I blow all they heads off. Then I let myself down and each and every one I stomp they balls. But one of them a teenage girl just the top of her head blown back. I commence giving it to her mouth when I hold her up by the shoulders. That was the best I ever had."

The room was as quiet as a tomb. Only Cruthers's voice was going and the cat never moved. This must have been going on a long time. Cruthers finished the story and went in the kitchen to make himself another drink. There were going to be a lot more stories.

I looked down to Bandini and he was staring at the floor with a smile. His eyes were wet and he was in a hypnotic region.

"*Feel* the turning and the twistings of all that, how Cruthers got there and the dispossessed without any mission but this rendezvous with a boy from Water Valley, Mississippi, and the gun he sleeps with in a tree, making love to it sixteen thousand miles from home. Nothing could stop it, nothing."

I was stunned by the new deep voice of Bandini, and this whole language.

When I looked at him again I believe he had forgotten I was in the room. He smiled just slightly and I could see how deeply in love he was.

Taste Like a Sword

WHY ARE YOU ALIVE? THEY ASK ME.

It's not the first time these two have been in here at that table almost in the street window there as you see. They march in and sit, light up, you bring them over that narrow plastic menu and they say Hello again. Why are you alive? The hateful thing is he looks just like me, the other one who doesn't talk much. But he searches my face for the answer, intent. Why *are* you alive? But he smokes and smokes, my old brand when I was a smoker. Their bicycles both lean together almost on the glass outside. I thought at first they were Mormon, that I was the only outlet for whatever meanness they had. But that wasn't so. They are no church.

Even a monkey can imitate life, the speaker says. Other creatures can be taught to make the gestures of a man. I saw a chicken in South Carolina once could count change, which you barely have to do. But you're coming along nicely. You've got the worthless café doper down almost exactly right.

The one who looks too much like me seems in a hurry with his glances, like, When are you going to get out of my way, out of everything's way, I wonder? The other says, It would seem nature gets lonely for moving life. God must be so lonely, such a party guy. Just something that treads by as an example, and you were elected for this space.

He points to this area of the café and makes both his hands walk across the tabletop. They could be two starfishes on a stage. You're not even a decent hole, he goes on. Why aren't you a woman? Then you might give some good man fifteen minutes' peace.

It's sort of a scandal you're a male, yes. For godsake do something about your face. We're eating here. Then he whispers: Where did you get the hair, where was that borrowed? I suppose to you your hair is somehow tragically significant and those shorts with your weenie legs and high-laced booties. Have you just come down off the mountain, dear friend, stamping out a forest fire, or have you just licked them with your spit and furred tongue? The other one just watches pale and with tired eyes like me. His clothes look like he bought them somewhere pricey though.

I think he will rise up and become me, absorb me, he is impatient for my space, is my feeling. But that must also mean there's something good about me he has to have, and my silence leaves me in a superior position. He seems very tired from watching. I'd think he's watched me at home too some way. The days keep going by and he just about has had it, is the feeling.

Across the room near the bar kneels Minnie Hinton. That same man is back at her table ordering his expensive whiskeys. Everything he does is costly. I believe he is a doctor going to law school in his Mercedes convertible. Something about the law and medicine and some field where you just sit on your butt being smart for high pay, as I understand. I believe there is a broomstick far up him. I sense the end knob of it is about at his Adam's apple in his throat in there. He moves off the axle of this long stick in him. He is short with square shoulders, square face, and some gray curls in his black hair like somebody near a condo pool looking sidelong at lesser creatures with open contempt. Thirty years ago where he lives they would call a pad. The disdain of this man is thick, is the feeling, with Minnie knelt there in front of him. He is moving ahead, always moving, down from his townhouse on the square and he resents he's on the ground with the others and having to walk where they walk, is my sense. It is my personal persuasion that he is taking it up the butt but he is frightened by this fact, he the doctor. You see others of his kind taking it up the butt and they trot around with a combination of fear and disdain, somebody on their trail, they have the best drugs, they must be quick. Minnie kneels down before him. She wrings her hands looking into his face. His face is quiet, almost without expression, but his mouth is moving all the time, whispering, you can barely hear anything over here with the crowd. He must know this. From him there is a long hiss that never quits.

Once you are tuned into the hiss you can define it clear as a bell out of the casual buzz of the whole eatery. This is eatery and bar both and they have good music at night, but I'm jealous of the musicians and it hurts to listen to them having fun. I like the bad bands better, the ones with stupid humor and little talent. They make me feel at home and I might stay through midnight even after waiting tables all day. The girl followers of bad bands are my kind too. They like it bad and true talent frightens them. They will go home with you sometimes not expecting anything and pull apart their poor clothes and fall to love like simple honest mechanics who've been prepaid for repairing a part. Then afterwards you just walk around with a slight crush on each other and maybe never even see them again except on the arm of a new loser but giving you a smile like everything is understood and cruising in its right orbit.

But Minnie's companion, who pays high for this act, is not casual. Things intended and designed pour out from him without stop, and it is the same Minnie, the goddess of this place and introduced to strange life by poverty, who fractures you in her quietness. She's almost on her knees but I suppose actually in a crouch before his knees with his hands on each like a priest speaking his best sermon. But she is pitched close to the attitude of the outright kneel.

Slut tramp whore rimsucker harlot Ford Escort blow job, he keeps going on as she listens calmly. Hag bitch scum. In the whisper, hardly a breath between.

Yes sir, she says.

Right as hell you swallow it all. Gutter lizard.

Yes sir.

Right now, come and die bitch, right now. Get off and die. I'll keep on while you're dead.

Then he shows just a flick of his rock-hard eyes down at Minnie's face. In that second you can see very sadly how much he wants to be her.

Netherson. I never meant to meet Netherson, who once for a whole week had nothing to eat in Amarillo, Texas. He slept in a park in Amarillo and played checkers for food with people better than he and always lost. The cops would come by rousting him from the park and other hard beds under trees near water. He was too weak to do much but sleep but he couldn't even finish a nap. The cops had his number, and he was black as a further kicker. He is something of a legend here, having missed many meals back then in his questing youth. He hit the road with absolutely nothing, which those who write about it never really do. He never had a dog companion. He was just himself and bone needy all over the West, Northeast, Midwest, and South, where he finally stopped when work opened. Netherson as a barman is a black zombie. He is moved by nothing, but he seems to be called by something, a voice is persistent in his forehead, you can almost see it in the wires of his temples. He is called away, he's not standing here, not looking at you. Some believe he's a god, especially the girls, he's somebody long ago crucified now back to show you his hands, the ones pushing the drink to you, no expression in his face, nothing.

I did not want to meet him. He scares me. But once I saw those dead eyes briefly come alive to some softness like a hamster's or a small child's. He scares me like something out of a sea bottom. Behind him the putty is flaking down at the bottom of the long bar mirror where the sunlight always hits with that *one* beam, just that one beam. A flashlight beam at the bottom of Netherson's sea and this disturbs me. People look at Netherson and laugh that laugh of deserted insides, very flat, no reaction from him. It occurs to me all the laughter here is like that. Even the two waiting for me to come back and get my treatment when I bring the order.

Minnie, almost to the full kneel like a woman in church, I think of her and Netherson getting naked together, for he is her man. That's hard to realize. She's his woman and you can't believe he ever asked for anything. Although I am ashamed and even cruel sometimes, I need to be with some woman, testament to my existence. Be in a suit have some money sell something travel. Somebody would sort of miss me. Netherson stuck on himself in his zombiehood. If my cat would die I could have freedom and a personality maybe but I love the cat. She reminds me there is not much to it, only the noise, and sleeps three quarters of the day.

The hands on the clock seem like snakes any minute to curl out and fall on your neck. But on my boots I can rise, I am solid, I can stand with Netherson, I have the soul of an implacable Negro. In certain moments, not many, I can reasonably imagine a tall naked woman standing there beside

me with her hand on my butt, saying, Yes I am all his. Sometimes I think about my mother's panties and where I came
from, place to place to place. She was tall and strong and
my father was in helicopter technology, a civilian hired by
different arms of the service. I was not curious enough to
ask much about him and now I realize he might have been
interesting although something about my devoted apathy in
my teens wouldn't let me like him. He loved it that helicopters packed the most punch in modern war. He was short,
but he stood tall on that fact, and he stood tall in lots of
places, Florida, Oregon, Delaware.

My mother would tremble at the window when he
was overhead in a helicopter. She was a nervous woman, but
tall and strong. Even nervous my mother was stronger than
my father. He was freckled with round shoulders but he had
fine fingers for his work and in Louisiana he received an
award on the tarmac near those tall pines and red dirt. The
pines had moss hanging down and I was back in a veil of it
pretending I was dead while the helicopters in the air went
by *pop pop pop* packing their punch. Much of what I see reminds me of death but death is interesting, not just sitting
there. It is red, green, and blue of dirt, pines, and sky, and
it is moving around, my mother being nervous there at the
window. Death was like Stalin moving behind the scenes
with a mustache killing every other person, Stalin the very
man my father opposed, as I gather. Yet he died and they
cut the brain out of his head to study.

I had a dream about Stalin in my room looking for
his brain. My mother was in the dream, still nervous, she
seemed to know where it was. My dead father was sailing
around the room showing everybody his lung cancer but
laughing at Stalin even though he hardly ever laughed when
he was alive. I want to be dead like Netherson, nothing in

my eyes, maybe be nothing but black muscle with eyes in it. Minnie would come to me. No more on her knees making extra money listening and agreeing. No more enduring this shame and this slackness and the total indifference of Netherson.

Death, let's get it on, I say.

Not so fast though.

Here we go again at my table. Look who's back, the lone wartberry, guy says.

While I'm holding the trays up, the man who looks like me except groomed has not said a word yet, but he has roll crumbs on his mouth and the white sauce of the salad remains in a line across his upper lip. He does not eat well, so impatient he is, while the other goes on.

We are sworn to bring the message home to you, Wartly. We *do* wish we could see your dreams. Most waiters are waiting until a better thing turns up. But you, Wartly, seem already promoted beyond your talents. This man speaking is courtly, of the world. Even his rich tie looks born for him, his shoes are loving animals gathered to his feet. When I brought him more tea, the meal had not tired him at all. He says, Our old pale old Wartly. Why *are* you alive? Could it be that *anyone* would find you necessary? We've figured you as a walking breathing missing person but nobody searching for you.

Yes *who*? The other man, even more like me suddenly, finally spoke. His look lingered on me. I could hardly believe he had spoken. He is moving up in my eyes and shoulders with his expression. He is taking possession, after long patience, in exasperation, is how it feels. I move away from myself into even further nothing, not toward death, not toward Netherson, and I float out the window, past Minnie Hinton still on her knees before her paying customer, always right, the hissing man, him set there in a pout, and I float out into the alley into the hot meat exhaust fan and pavement oil with my arms around the Dumpster, is how it feels.

I could be Fagmost, on the other hand. He is that drunkard always sick under the stands after every ball game, puking up his guts but smiling. He screams at the team for three solid hours and then you will see him dancing alone in the lowbrow clubs around town. You see him on his hands and knees but making kick motions like a dancer shot down. Then one night two policemen piled into the crowd and dragged Fagmost off, him all wet in his lumpy flower shirt and dirty beard. He never claimed to be nice like everybody around here aspires to. I am nice, I am all right. What a nothing to be said, no? Why, he turned on the television just to get another herd of foreigners to scream at. He fed stray cats is the best thing I know about him. I could be him, but I doubt I have the staying power to be a good drunkard. You see Fagmost trying to eat a hearty meal, the way his lips quiver and he scrapes around at it, this man can move you with his lack of memory and gut persistence. He is smiling, mostly, and you see him back under the stands of the football stadium, puking without a thought of the well-dressed women around him and all the while wearing his smile. My Lord if I, say, had a good four-year war behind me and was a hopeless lush carried down the street by a flock of children on Memorial Day, that would be something like Fagmost, that would be Fagmostian, I wouldn't have to stand for any of this over at that table. Nobody wants to take the time to insult Fagmost, he is so out there.

But I just want to eat candy and drink three sodas with it then fall asleep with a sweat on me watching some women prisoners in slips on the television, wanting to be their guard. I would even wear a slip too just for fun because all women know how to talk. I would like to have a poison ivy rash and have them scratch it for me, all in their slips and their little folkways to cure what ails you.

Or I could be Jimmy with Mr. Beckett in the alley. Jimmy wears a football helmet and Mr. Beckett follows him with a cane. They are inseparable. Jimmy pigeon-toed and hunchbacked. He gimps along slowly looking at the pavement, while Mr. Beckett follows. Then he will strike Jimmy over the helmet with the cane, *blap*, and there you are their never-ending street playhouse. Jimmy goes into a howling fit to remark on his discomfiture and sends Mr. Beckett down to hell several times. Then Mr. Beckett extends his hand, apologizes. They make up and move on to drink coffee in the town café across the street under a marlin on the walls. They are feebleminded but they have structure and design such as discussed in that class at the U I took. Wouldn't you imagine Mr. Beckett is a god, and Jimmy, looking for cans to cash in, his faithful servant? While I serve and yet never serve anything.

While the two are finishing up their meal I don't have to look over there. I can feel that one's eyes on my back. The clock is hard to watch too the way it is rushing forward and the hands trying to get out like snakes. It is hot on my back and the one at the table is running after me down a gray alley with the air heavy in hot meat exhaust every damned pizza ever consumed like preflatulence of the eating mobs. I'm out of breath just turning around and my bare legs over my boots look like thin milky sticks to run on, they can't carry on much farther, I should have done more exercise like God intends for real men only I'm in love with my weakness, women in slips could stand and lie all around me licking my disease, they go for weak men you know, oh yes they love

nothing better than a bad poet who needs all kinds of help
and understanding even to finish out a new poem about self-
abuse. The man handles me somehow, yes his fingers go
around my neck become snakes off the clock, next the way
he steps into me with his knees behind my knees, paralyz-
ing me to make me buckle like somebody collapsed in love.
He is like smoke and he wears me like a suit or maybe just
underwear.

My mother, the strong one, taller than both my father
and me, she was always at the window nervous, looking out
at the flatness of the airfields where my father worked. She
said she wondered why we needed to go to the moon, we
already lived on it, we had lived on many moons, one moon-
scape to the next. They are making my mind flat, she said,
and she never complained much. My tits are going flat, my
breast does not swell, no heart in it I can see out there honestly try as I might, then try to love again in another place,
wherever God has furnished another pool table for their little
games. You can't just peer out to the flats forever. I can't
love again, I can't. You will have to make do with some
younger gypsy with huge breasts. Even in her depression my
mother was strong, you see. But she pitied me and all the
ones over the world who were never quite dead but little else.
That is the trouble with everything, she said, new people are
not quite loved like I can't quite love you or your father. On
the streets in the airports in the churches in the stores they
are not quite loved. You can see it in almost everybody's eyes.
They are paying for somebody to love them, they are trying
to make up somebody who loves them, but everybody's soul
is stretched out flat, we just are things to sit something on
like airfields. There are too many places too many pictures.
Nobody can get to them except crazy people like my own

father your granddaddy. He was crazy but he taught me to love and be loved.

My father, I just remembered. He was working on a strange gas with a space name to power a weapon that in a single helicopter you had the gunforce to level a block in Manhattan at midnight in a storm. He worked always deep into the night even at home and he loved those Winston cigarettes. When he was diagnosed with lung cancer his doctor suggested he sue the government because that space gas had a direct bearing and he the doctor would testify so. But see this, my father was a patriot as well as a small genius and he could not in good heart as he put it, and with cancerous lungs as he could have, sue his own government even if it would provide millions and Harvard for me and a palace in the mountains for my mother although my mother always said she just wanted one small Ozark to live on at last, she was from Arkansas and that's all she dreamed of, just the one little mountain. So he just blamed the Winstons alone and nobody knew of the other until his partner later died too with tumors like fists in his head and lungs and liver.

The very next day after my father was diagnosed, I mean the next day after that ceremony on the tarmac, helicopters saluting him from overhead in a squadron, I watched where he got the award. In Louisiana. The moss hung from the limbs of the pines and the sun up like bright hell, the sky just stupid and blue, a skinny squirrel running behind the grandstand over the tarmac like some rat making a protest, all that pavement and *bop bop bop*ping metal sound overhead. Before he began crying and getting smaller, he said, Yes, there are too many. God bless war otherwise the pestilential hordes reaching up to level us. There you'd really have your flat plains. You can never trust an armed corporal, boys and girls, something's different there no matter what you read. Trust this, history will always create a monster to harvest the millions. We should worship the helicopter, boy, god of our times, Hitler Stalin Mao, Hussein, all of them corporals. There is not even such a thing as a personal soul in many countries. The souls were dead already waiting for Marx, all he was was the final announcement. I am dying for you, I have had hell so you may carry on. Love me, every breathing motherfucker around me. I give you my lungs and heart to eat thereof. I taste like a sword.

When I turn to take the bill over, the man who looks just like me is standing right in my face. His meal is all in his breath.

Isn't it time we met? he asks. Please take off that apron.

Repulsed

WHEN THE DETECTIVE COMES HE IS NEVER WHAT YOU WOULD think at all. The questions aren't fair as you'd presume. But his gun and cigarettes are very long. They become enormous batons eventually. And my gracious the boots. They are like elegant scrollworked skis and the points on them could flatten a roach in a corner. As he remonstrates you feel that more honestly he would kick you in both eyes with them and slide in your blood.

For many years I was quiet. I did not talk, I had nothing to say long—millennia, it seemed—after the event of my puberty. I did not quite all shut up, not enough, because when my words went out they were worthless, mere agreement with the village wisdoms so that I could occupy my rented space without trouble. It's the confidence that he is renting space, no more, that marks the foreigner, whereas the loud citizens call out as if rooted to favorable ground in a fort with hooting windows. I prayed to be firm, I prayed to be even sullen in my adolescence. But I was too much the blown leaf cracked dry under their boots, not even ignored. At the end I begged strong drink and large women to relieve me, just as I had while an urchin begged the walnut orchard to let go and smite me with those heavy nuts in their pods. Help me, touch me. I wished for women on bicycles to race to me with their hair like ragged wings, flying. I begged for that but could barely find my voice.

But once, playing my forlorn old trumpet, can't it be forgiven that I saw her through the bare limbs of the tree next to my house in its March agony, into where the woman

153

was, not on a bicycle come to snatch me up, but an older woman? Only in night dreams could I abide her. She was eating an enormous piece of bread, I thought, the whole loaf of French bread. It was so large it looked to be a separate thing delivered to her out of her drapes. A buttered French bread afloat there at her lips.

Long, long afterwards, long beyond that moment I held at my belly my old trumpet tasting of wet zinc, long after the woman seated almost clothed there through the bare notch of the early March limbs, past the years I drank enough to talk, then got gnawed by every wrong kind of woman there was, gnawed and thrashed by their awful stories (because I made them tell all to learn what being rightly human was about, even the woman who kept marrying others while we were courting I made tell everything before she got off her bicycle); on past this I only half realized what I had seen. Can't I be pardoned, because what ecstasy holds a candle to the sudden intelligence one is granted years, whole cycles of war and famine, after viewing a rare event in ignorance? The collision of mind and flesh, all your veins pumped with light. Your own sweet innocence brings tears to your eyes, which see again revised, nostalgia on you like a barrel of walnuts. Time has been a kind uncle saving your inheritance until the moment was right. He has been patient, his hands out to you over the years. The woman's husband was a rented soul too, in our neighborhood of pale clerks in their red brick dormings. He too was dull. He came to this town where nobody would ever ask him, How could you deserve this wife of yours? Drudge as you are, teacher of religious education, you must have rich hidden gifts, eh? This town with a surplus of flanking churches where the unctuous and the grim were sanctified. No ruffians took him off to the alley and told him, Your face is getting on our nerves, see, gray

fool. While I played my trumpet at all their studied vener-
able blank heads, unable to speak.

   After that afternoon their marriage somehow ground
to a halt, a halt of a halting anyway, and a muted scandal
hung around them when he went away. I would have known
everything, had I known. She was Mediterranean, a little
anyway, although her voice was the same as everyone's.
Some Sicilian, maybe, frowning out of her. Or she could be
a tropical Jewess. I thought I had driven them apart with my
trumpet and was vain. In three separate sleeps I dreamed of
her and I was ruined for the regular girls. I couldn't speak
to them anyway. At every pass I was vanquished except in a
state contest where they gave me a yellow ribbon for superior.

   Then I went to the nationals where I was attacked
by a Latvian judge and driven into the familiar dark again,
where a bum with perfect pitch heard me and mugged me
of my instrument. But I lingered there in New York and
drank out the tanks of this my first metropolis. I felt I was
on the last planet of man, where the dregs of all stories were,
and I became for years a mere roving hole of audiation, a
great ear in my courtly brogans rubbed off to the white
underneath.

   When I finally got my story out, the woman and the
loaf, it had a terrible design to it, and the terrible part confused others. What terrible, how terrible, why terrible? Or was
my story really kind, perhaps tragic too, the loaf floating out
of her curtain, the man's head in the curtain, he wore the
curtain, wasn't I remembering that finally? This was my first
anecdote but I couldn't blurt it out correctly. I didn't have
the light yet. The conjunction was not quite made, I had not
driven the thing home. I was a sorry sight to my ruined acquaintances, shouting in my liquor, Show it, prove it, let's have
it out in the open! Drinking my cheap scotch, shouldering

through mongrel New York. Or worse, meeting my own kind. It's a hideous affront to see your own kind on the walks there. You want to run into them, through them, blaming them for the needless duplication. There they are with their own loyal monkeys around them, redundantios.

Nevertheless I went on searching for my trumpet. I had met the man who stole it many, many times, but he never recognized me. He wore a hat like my father's except much taller in the crown, perhaps ten inches of hat there giving him away and the further clue that he had never moved from the spot where first he fell on me, but without the trumpet in his hands now. My trumpet old and zinc flavored but mine and a partner to my vision through the naked tree. But this man begged so violently I couldn't just stand there accusing him with my new New York voice. No, he would get the jump on you begging so you felt he'd tear your limbs and clothes off for a dime, and *he* saw no redundancy in people, he was such a consumer, so needy. He begged the same man as yesterday, who always gave something to him. He would beg the same man over and over, each day freshly minted, unbeggared. People gave him buttons, Tums, lint, keys, all over again. During his racket I was trying to get a word in but at not too close range. He had sucked in my horn and I felt did not remember this. Besides, he was pure. I mean he barely acknowledged the turds and string thrown at him. It was begging itself, the clean form, he aspired to. I tell you there was not the least suggestion he was mad. You saw a great patient sanity in his eyes under the hat, a sort of rage. Now and again he broke into song, always sweetly pitched, almost angelic like a castrato. I believe the whole street thought him superior, I'd swear it. They feared him when the cold days began and he became even louder, fearless, their obliviousness

sorely tested. With more cold he loomed more awful, a fiend
let down off a bronze horse rampant with pigeons and green
mange. He kept up in his thin, not too nasty, clothes, a suit
with vest over a tuna gym shirt. On his cheeks were handsome small tracks of acne. This touched me, his old teen-
agehood shared with mine. With his persistence in the thin
clothes under the tall optimistic hat as the chill of the mongrel city went inward to your marrow, then grew like a vine
around your feet. I began to love the man.

It started in pity as I saw him huddle, then hunker,
some special wind from Maine smashing his pride. But he
ascended to a racket of beseeching every now and then.
Hardly anybody knew me, but I knew him. All the iron in
me fled as love took over. Love is a buttered clarinet, that's
what it is. You've barely touched the instrument but begin
your wretched toots on the alien thing.

Sir, I said, Sir, don't you have my horn? If so, just
keep it, don't think a thing about it. Or you could give it
back. Either way your heart desires. I spoke aloud.

The cold in him gave me my brief opportunity. He
was not quick enough to drown me out begging. Holy God,
the man collapsed when he heard me. On the spot he fell
inwards. You saw what a delicate thing his need was. Re-
versed, begged at, he suffered spasms of revolution. Under
the ambitious hat you saw the woe of an artist gripped in
bankruptcy.

The horn, devoured so long ago, the idea of the
horn pitched him into such a rage about every delinquency
of the planet he could not finish yelling them out. He could
not possibly announce all that was owed him. He broke
down in a sickness of decomposition. I was a heinous agent
from the Outer and his beany eyes magnified me. He shrank
in his thin suit. He was a dog rolled over in awe, spreading

his legs to explain his inconsequence. His protests died choking.

Say, there's not that much to it, man. We could let it go. It's just I've waited so long, the months of growing this beard on my face, I said.

He jumped towards me and put his hands around my throat. But then he shrank back in his suit odor. The odor was not that bad, either that or I had become married to it in my long wait for the horn.

The philosopher had it right, the monkey scratches its fleas with the key that opens its cage. I was liberated to speak by the whiskey but more by the bum, while he dove back in his cage at the horror of being asked for anything back. The whirlpool of need stopped cold by a simple request.

He ran off somewhere and then was here again. I had the old horn back in my hands, just a shade greener with corrosion, and I was free to see my youth again. From then on he would hardly look at me until one day he and the hat were immobilized by sleet. I think he was dead or very ill, squatted there in a stare. Maybe he was me in my old age. I didn't want to age anymore up north. I took a bus driven nearly walking speed back to my own rented lands.

In the warmth I got a temper on me, in my old town much the same except they sold more whitened lawn turd and the billboards had taken over the air crying Money! It was hard to go back to my room because the woman still lived over there darker, and her hair streaked with gray, very long and neglected. The rumor was that alone, she hardly left her chair. I was not prepared to see her in the very same chair, in the exact old place, the vista through the tree obscured by the leaves of spring. I had a temper now, though, I was advanced. I could be, finally, sullen. My life's work was ahead of me. Now was not the time for sullenness. The leaves should not have made me so angry. I was having my sullen stage inappropriate to my season. My region was covered in leaves, steaming leaves and giant insects and cats screeching as they mated, infamy proceeding regardless of the churches and their desperate parking flats swept clean to the point of cruelty. Beating back nature was the obsession of men in these suburbs, and failing that, arranging it like a combed orphan. But you could wake up here with new vines in your room like criminals.

In my absence my parents had gotten a dark orange boxer bitch. They had more affection for the animal than me, but that didn't upset me. I wanted alone in my work whenever I found it. The dog went around the house hiding meal bones in cushions and nooks. This delighted the folks. Look at her, such a steward! Why can't you be such a steward? This was their favorite parable from Scripture, the Good Steward. But I got home so poor I was wearing my pa's shirts rolled up at the sleeves.

For a while I was excused as a patient in need of food and exercise. I seemed weaker than I was. I brought an old typewriter from the back porch to my room. Here I practiced letterheads for my work, toiling through several choices. A position I could hurl all my resources at, but I had none much, only fear and indignation until I settled on church trumpet. Within the day I was combing my hair differently and carried my letterheads from room to room, trailed by the orange boxer who wanted me for a friend.

My folks went all out as if this was the last gift to me and bought me a new horn. I would take myself to huge wealthy churches with their mobs of penitents. The woman, sitting in her chair, while the brown toasted loaf floated to her, out of the curtain it seemed, until I recalled the husband's near-bald head above in it—I used this mystery in my horn and had new tones. Many horns, hundreds, were in the Scriptures, I reasoned. They would see I was necessary. I would be history walking in, an old friend.

But just now with the folks out, I went out to the tree where it was wet from rain and cut the leaves back for the notch, such a hallowed ordinary thing to be doing in these suburbs. I wore Pa's big rubber boots. We had a long trimmer for the job and I never looked away until I exhausted my steward's duty. But when I appeared again in my room I was naked except for the boots and the new trumpet at my belly, feeling this was how the Hebrew trumpeters of old were, they must have been. In my work. My hair was fresh from the rain and recombed in my new way. In my horn would be the beggar of New York too. And the orange dog with her belligerent adoration.

Older and darker, she was in the chair, which had been turned a little, more toward me, so that half her face might be watching me from its one eye. I in my maturity. She looked the age of a matron doing the rumba in a film I had long ago endured. They whispered she was now either a drunkard or had been lamed by a stroke. I was late, so late. So like me to turn up just in time for despair. You know the type. Several ambulances had come and gone at her place, the word was. But I begged, again the beggar, Let that which remains reveal itself, Let there be a spark of health still in her. Let my music enter her to assuage our loneliness. All she had to do was give me some sign. She had been in my dreams waking and sleeping for so long. My youth sobbed at her window. Help me, where were you? How could you live through that afternoon and have nothing more for me? You are famous in your rousing obscurity for many wretches and their duplicates in New York. For you I have borne the tale without quite having the message. Here, with my combed hair, look! I shouted through my open window. Grown, my voice no longer had that ugly wayward whine. I felt I was succeeding. This house was cast loose in this rain like a wild brick boat and I was in the wheelhouse. We were nosing into the swells. Ahoy. I with my profession. She in her enigma my woman. I was finally deep in the world, like the beggar and the others I envied.

I didn't go on forever. I couldn't be sure she'd ever looked even as I began playing my trumpet. In the manner of Gideon at sea, those hours until my lips went to blubber. And Jonah spat up onshore, returned in his ministry to our difficult homeland.

Although she never said so, I believe Mother had taken a job since I was in the house. Sometimes she was away weeks, so in essence the house was mine. When she returned it was in every case that she caught me in the act going about various manipulations at the window. Consider her punctuality, the unmitigated shame of this, for after all I was grown. It was as if she stayed under the house and came up only when she heard noises. I was not yet going to the churches, going about my internship there. She was promptly in the room from nowhere suddenly, myself a wincing wreck. There's never really time to develop one's ambitions. They just throw you out there and you grab on to something handy like an amateur, in terror. Hardly time to hide your cheap scotch and prepare a face. Pa, for instance, had chosen wrongly, rushed to life insurance when he wanted to be a cowboy, then panicked by my advent, my whirling hole of needs. Forced into his lies: I love you, love you, boy. It was grievous, but he still managed in his sentimental way to be gone huge lengths of time like a star of the rodeo. I see my pa sitting in his parked car for hours looking at true horsemen in a lot somewhere, bewitched and sad.

In my case nothing prepared me for my success. Outside my window two blue jays ebbed and flowed and made their hoarse quacks only for me, I pretended.

The first minister was no fool, he agreed immediately, and to a handsome figure that left me filthy with cash relative to the none I'd had yesterday. I played from a projection booth in the balcony through the hole where religious films were projected, big epics of the waddling masses under the Hebrew kings and their antagonists. The man believed devoutly in old Hollywood, especially Debra Paget in her golden halter. He didn't count much on the abstract. He was thoroughly for the age of vision come again after two millennia's trifling with print and its craven black and white. Next to the rolling wheels aloft, I blew during the films and even afterwards, antiphonal to the choir in the loft below, at last let make their own noise until everybody filed out and I was left alone with the hot machine. You could not see much from the projection slot except the minister in his pulpit to the right of the screen all thrilled and bent forward like a longbow and seized by his approving spasms. The people went out into the street, chatting gulls driven off an argosy. He succeeded in bringing in more of the young. I was partly responsible. I had the impression of motion through the universe, very happy there in my elevated box. Ahoy. I once owned a happy cat named Ralph who would rush out to meet people, calling to them. This was how I felt, like Ralph with his salutations, for the first time in my life.

Other Sundays I pressed forth, there is no rest in the professions once engaged, down to the ocean where a priest thought I was essential. I was in the ramparts instead of an organ they could not afford. It was a poor church although very pretty. A submerged cartoon in blue, white, green, and orange. Already I had broken my earlier rule to stick with the rich Christians. Maybe I was becoming a little Christian myself. It's hard to tell. The priest felt very puny beneath all the colors and really, he was, with his grim whispers. He was trying for more balls, as he put it, in himself and service. I was instructed to play freeform at any inspired moment even while he talked or whenever I felt there was a lapse in worship. I was so good at this a very old man thought I was a violin. Then it was nice to go down wading in the sea and believe in God, to pretend I had girlfriends and deep acquaintances, like poor Pa with his cows and salty pals.

Back at the house I lent Pa money and stared with my new power through the notch of the tree outside my window.

But one day the curtain was closed.

Great God, they always dig the tunnel right where you love, don't they? Somehow they have known the route all along, then they are right next to you, plundering jackals, bothered spies eating toward your heart in their envy, fiends with cutting nails and their dread offices. Just at your high tide too, everything smiling, your old parents in your hands like glass animals; the orange bitch humping herself, so glad for your arrival.

He was a relative of hers, a detective, he said, wearing an even bigger hat than the beggar and as in Pa's dreams, his boots and long gun. You could see Pa crumpling in envy.

With my parents gathered at our eating table, he continued.

In essence, you killed her, he says. With her stroke, she could not take her eyes away from you. Neither stop your nasty suggestive horn playing every tune she most abhorred.

The whole point of her later life in fact was to escape wherever horns were. She only wanted a little liquor and great silence, poor thing.

I did not, could not, I said.

Mother witnessed against me.

Next Pa crept from his station of hunched envy. Might I have a look at your peacemaker there under the coat? he wondered.

Stand back, little missus, warned the man. After much unbuckling came out his exquisite almost interminable gun, practically a hand rifle. Unduly long and quarrelsome in its chromium. Then it was back in his coat, snapped into harness, a cruel aid to his searches and legal destruction. Pa was stunned as by a miracle snatched away in full bloom.

The man wore provocative and immense boots too. Sort of a dancing cream leather boot poured on the end of his heavy legs.

After the end you still kept on, the man scolded me. She must have been gone in the chair two days, three, while you went on mocking her.

How could you know?

You were at it even as they discovered the body. This looked to be such a decent lovely neighborhood. However.

He stared at me all over again, refreshed by pure loathing.

In my line of work you seem to find at least one monster in every block. A sorry rule, but one without which I wouldn't be necessary at all. There isn't hardly any kind of human ugliness can live by itself forever. It can't keep, it's got to leap out on parade. Then they call me.

How wonderful, said my pa, the borrower.

Who sent you? I asked. I deny everything. It was her fault, when I was young. She ate floating bread. You weren't there.

Here is the evidence by witness: you switched from an old horn, a bent one, to a new one even shriller and more bombastic. Is this the case? He put away his notes.

It is, said my mother. He resumed.

You can't obscure this in mysticism. Your "floating bread." When you were young. You were hardly a juvenile when you finished her.

Bread, long brown bread floated toward her face from out of the curtains, I swore.

Wonderful and sad, my pa spoke again. I should have known, so instantly feral and willing to attack the first wounded among us.

There will probably be a fine, which I might get reduced, since you two in your ignorant disgrace, have, I feel this deeply, been the salt of the earth, *ignorant* of this man's troubles.

We are ignorant, said Pa. You can't know.

The man recited a tale of another's crime so vile and lethal they were relieved in the comparison. Such tears of innocence gathered in Mother's eyes I could have smashed her. Now I seemed merely a squalid pile they could talk around.

There it is, that's how they find your route and burrow right into your works. The ruin of your ambitions, your virtues, love's persistent dream. The orange boxer bitch turns its butt to you, slinks off with your kin, the shocked traitors. Next the imposition of a monstrous fine all of them agree is most lenient. I would be ruined for years along with my father. He was so happy, Mother and he without hope, at last, after the niggling prospects, the ray sent back from the future now and then. Finally a tragic humiliation from which there was no recovery.

I never had even time to mourn her. They took it away.

Then I was cashiered by the pastor and priest both, because the old begging had crept back into my tone. The protestations of a swatted rooster, this tone, which drove some of their sheep, they swore, into the arms of atheist gloom.

Left with memories of the sea, but like a slug launched into low tide never to swell in my horn work again, oh no. They know you.

It hardly matters now what I have paid in coin of words, angry reader, or what I have paid in time and money until a few years ago my breakout, my wives and wealth, my long hard pistol of a car. One wife hardly ever left the car, as I pressed her further and further into relating every morsel, leave nothing out. Hearing enough descriptions of other men, I finally borrowed a personality for my own.

An altogether different tale. Rest assured however that no lush ecstasy, no minutes of sweet confusion, have ever come near the woman seated in the chair, that green shawl down on her shoulders, bare, and the long bun aloft, nearing her face. She was so startled as she prepared her mouth for it, wider and wider. After that, ruin and our haunted fellowship.

But I remember she was dazzled looking up in the curtains at the bald man's approach through a raised single drape colored purple. She wore an amazed smile on her face suddenly as she complied.

After all, my life has been a slow and mistimed one, but it is good, good, I testify, even at the bottom of my melancholy. I dare you to argue with me, digusted counselors. You never had a joy nearly so fine.

Two Gone Over

I was in North Dakota around the SAC base in March. The wind blew hard across the beetfields and the tarmac, wherever it was. I had done my duty in Grand Forks and we talked in a bar. She and her girlfriend were both in cowboy boots. The woman I was interested in had very excellent calves. Her face was high cheekboned with huge eyes like china marbles. Her forehead was touched around by brown bangs that made my stomach ache. She was a Florida beauty, Tallahassee, just a slight quarter inch heavy with winter flesh, that's all, a slight quarter inch.

I told her she was the one who broke my heart in high school and made me cry on my pillow. She was the type. Little Anthony and the Imperials sang about her. I loved Little Anthony because he could gasp so good, he wrung it all.

Later, when I was alone with her, she said she wasn't really that type. She was a simple Southern girl, but her father was Satan. We were in those couples apartments near the SAC base. The apartment was similar to rooms I had down South when I was first a bachelor, divorced. But they were even smaller and poorer, with a feeling of transience, little attempt at decoration.

My home woman and I had become, I think, old friends more kindly than passionate. In fact she was still married although long separated. We had hung together in a vast common loneliness almost like love. I liked to see her onstage in a gown playing her flute in the orchestra, very well. She had a doctorate from Boston University, which I understand is something.

She had lent me some money in a humiliating emergency, and now in Grand Forks I had a check in my pocket. I could repay her and I felt square, decent, and very American all of a sudden, as when you leave a gym with your hair seriously combed, wet, and walk into the cool evening. The earth is glad to see you.

The girl from Tallahassee was only twenty-four. I was forty-two.

She showed me album after album of B-52s in the air and on the ground. Her husband had wanted to be a fighter pilot but had not come up to the mark when he left Colorado Springs, the academy. I didn't mean to be ugly but I thought this was boring, the sky and the bombers, the ground and the bombers, the squad and the bombers. I might have said this. But she thought they were beautiful and told me so again and again. She was divorcing her husband, who was in the air now, but she thought the B-52s were exquisite. She wanted something beautiful in her life, these pictures, and I should not have commented at all, especially since her father was the Devil and she did not have him either.

After the tour through the photos I told her I ought to go back.

This is not turning out like I wanted it to, she said.

Well, this is your home, your married home. I couldn't possibly do anything here, don't you understand? Their married bed, and besides the husband might come in from an aborted mission. She could understand that, couldn't she? I couldn't have her here.

But—looking back—maybe her point was to have it here, right here. Don't be fast, be slow, she insisted. Right in the middle of the B-52 pictures. However, we drove in her car back to the motel. Crying cold black wind outside, all over Dakota.

I knew it would be like this, I could imagine, she said when we were in my room. She was downcast. I felt sorry for her. My clothes were strewn around. I didn't care for the look either, although I had never planned on much in this town. I wanted her in an almost crippling way now. It seemed more urgent with the black wind out there. Don't be fast, please. Just don't be fast, all right? she asked me.

You have other experiences?

No, only with my husband Nicholas. Now you.

By this time I was flooded with gratitude. I was little but a token offered in her satisfaction. I did not quite understand this. I did not want to be greedy. Her face all this while was never ironic, always sincere. She had set about this evening with conviction. I could hardly believe it, but we were becoming friends, and I found this very arousing.

I'm a little old for you, I guess.

No. What, forty-five?

Only forty-two. She thought I was even older and it seemed not to matter in the least. I may have been in my last blaze of attraction, whatever it was. But I could hardly believe my fortune. I began feeling sorry for her husband. Nicholas, she said, not Nick. Lumbering around the sky, obsolete.

In my memory, she was at school and in airports, peeling me with her eyes, just a few seconds, then turning and gone on her belly-dropping legs, off to better zones. She was the girls I could never have, in one. Then too I was having the air force and all the frigid black wind of the Dakota night, all that black wind between the places you have left behind that don't want you anymore.

All over America from shore to shore such lovely women as this marry too soon because somebody wants them too much. They are wanted so much they can't deny the hunger. The loves are too hungry and quick, the men fall on them and ravish them and use up the love almost instantly. They must eat every part. Then nothing is left, only two husks with their manners and they are just sitting there together glum and naked in the hats of their choice, not another word to say, not a drop left to give. Nature is through with them for a long while, and they begin friction over nothing, except that each feels cheated, always cheated, cheated every minute. Somebody once told me, as a thought in consolation, when you see a beautiful woman, always remember: Somebody is tired of her. Like most advice this is probably true and absolutely useless except to the wise dead. The dead sit around us in their great hats, nude, yammering away nevertheless.

I have felt of consequence to the universe only while drunk or at the moment of orgasm. These are lies too, I know, but good ones, an inkling. Maybe next for me is prayer, but with her I was praying only not to be too fast. She had drunk three wines at her apartment while going through the photos, I nothing for a long while now. Now she was lying naked on the bed, heavy breasts with dark exhuberant paps, her head propped on one arm, facing me under her pixie-cut hair with her high cheekbones, cheerful even though we were not lying on the B-52 pictures.

I was thinking of all that black wind outside the motel window, with her lying in the wind, only her. I saw nothing else in the room, just her and black rushing air around her. It was wonderful, this picture, but with an edge of terror too, an image come alive out of regular life. The wind was screaming and her husband's big plane, the size a football field, was screaming through and breaking up.

When I was with her I did not have her so much as melt twice inside. My word, I became a woman in her, is what it felt like. All the excitement, the hard passion from her place to here—I was sighing as if penetrated and then wrung out. Never in my life before, nothing like this. I would tell only you this, pal. I have nothing to boast about, nothing to leer at, I promise. No, there was hardly any pride. She was all the power, every minute of lost lechery in my life, a sucking dream in a black wind.

But when she left the room, she still smiled as if she were my friend, everything was lovely. I felt unsatisfying, my spine was vapor. She had admired my body, but I was the chew toy of a dog, pal, a sad man. I had wanted too much, I think, waited too long. I had dragged her back to the motel. This was wrong. So was her apartment wrong. There was no good place, there was no right place for us.

In the airplane home to Memphis I tried to raise myself, have my esteem back. For a few minutes I would recall her beauty and then boast inside, but this went away fast. Then I tried to attach a profound narrative to myself.

My uncle, a laughing athletic monument of a man, had mysteriously gone down in his B-26 while chasing Rommel in North Africa. For years my mother waited for news of her brother. In my infant memory I recalled her crying for him, didn't I? His widow was a delta beauty who remarried an important man, maybe a college president. I would see the two of them pictured in the paper. She stayed fine looking for at least thirty years. I admit to strange family thoughts about her. At fifteen I imagined that one day she would call me up and have me over to show me the ropes, in honor of my uncle's memory. All this was fitting for his nephew, perhaps even decreed in the Old Testament. They were twenty-three when my uncle disappeared. The woman of Grand Forks was twenty-four. She acted as if all this were inevitable. Witness our easy, instant friendship. Said I must see the bombers, must see how beautiful they were. We would have toiled in the photographs of the bombers. This was a profound narrative.

But it wouldn't stick, although I tried. I wanted badly to be a part of weeping history but the ghosts in this thing would not line up. Every now and then I would catch myself in a gasp, even a sob. Something was overcoming me, a kind of weak shame.

Life went on with my woman back home, but not for long. She left teaching at the college for banking, which was the profession of her father, a grim man in a characterless brick town on a hill in east Texas. I went around town dopey. The words *fill me, fill me* came to my lips constantly without my will. This would have been frightening but I was not that alert. I saw her play flute with the Tupelo Symphony a last time when an old man—once a master, I guess—was featured at the piano in a Gershwin concert. Either my ears had gone totally out or the man was simply possessed and awful. He thrashed on the keys way too loud and without sense. The audience sat there as if everything were sweet and ordained, but couldn't they hear that this old man in tails was awful? He might not even be the musician they invited. He might be someone deranged, an understudy who had killed the master and was now mocking him. Was I the only one appalled? I kept listening, then I suddenly saw him naked in a tall hat. A nude hatted monster, banging down with closed fists. Nobody around me reacted, of course. It was a sorry thing, and again, I would have been frightened, but I was dull as if doped.

Finally I could not stand this feeling anymore and went on a bender, after a year without a drink. I dragged the woman away from her commencement duties and took her to a reservoir in the northeastern corner of the state near Tombigbee. I imagined the woodsy rocks and bluffs with a cold stream down the middle. We never found this, a place I thought very necessary, very much an emergency. The cool wet rocks and mountain laurel with fish to catch. I conceived of our eating fish and living off the land, a rebaptism of ourselves. My fishing rods lay helter-skelter in the back of the car. But there was no proper place, then the moment was gone and I was just a fool. We stayed in a motel with thin pseudowood walls owned by Pakistanis, the poor woman exhausted, her last loyalty expired. I couldn't sleep well, and when I did I dreamed a number of the tall naked dead in extravagant hats, standing about like cattle.

Within the month, the woman got an abortion as I waited in the car. It was early on. I think I cared more than she did. She had never had children and didn't want any. Then, out in Texas while she worked in her father's bank beginning her new future, she met a blond man of new interest. I wrote to her but she didn't write back. I smelled something wrong and went on another bender, using every room in my house, a huge rented country estate—modest to be sure—to have pretentious toddies in. I was intent on finding the safe and happy mix. No sick loonies this time, surely not.

In the midst of this the girl in North Dakota called and said her divorce from Nicholas was accomplished. She was headed back South and would drop by on her way to Florida. This was good, I was happy. There may be something serious here. I smiled in my mansion under the oaks, my dogs racing around the yard beneath the giant magnolia. Christ, I was baronial, you couldn't stop me, man of many parts, hear, old son?

When she came in the house I was in a Confederate cavalry hat. I have no clear idea why, except I had become also a pilot. I could not refuse the conviction I was a fighter pilot. The hat gave me a certain authority, I felt. The passion of my race ran high in me. I talked in this vien while she sat and watched. She had lost weight and was all sunbrowned and lithe. I spoke directly into her black eyes, unconstrained, possessed. She seemed charmed and amazed. My powers wanted out of me. I could not hold them back.

I had a long drink in the kitchen, staring out at my rented orchard. The future looked bright now with missy in the house. Yes, there would be great carrying on. When I returned she was gone.

My nephew walked through.

Who was that? That was the best-looking woman I've seen in my life. Now she's just up and gone. Didn't even get her name.

Old son, you fool. Don't you understand she'll be back? She has no choice, I told him.

I got a letter from her in Florida. Who *are* you? she began.

It couldn't have occurred to me then, and didn't for another year, that I must have been, in my cavalry hat, a lunatic older version of the very man she had left behind in the air force. Even days after she left I could not quit being a pilot. I woke up in the mode.

Then the other collapse of that summer. A butchy wife and her namby husband, lawyers, bought the rented estate right out from under me. I had to pile my belongings into a two-story hovel next to a plowed field, an instant reversal from baron to sharecropper. My nephew had to drag me out of a bar where I was attempting to buy a coed with a roll of hundreds. My ex-woman was driving around town with her new smiling blond Texas boyfriend. She had changed the locks of her doors. I lost my driver's license. I went broke.

I could not eat, I went to the doc for depression. I was a wraith. Once, after some business in San Diego, as a passenger from the Memphis airport to home I was arrested for drunken riding. I have a clear memory of the dream I had those few hours in jail. The naked dead, all in hats and a foot taller than I, were in the jail cell. They said nothing. But they were mute with decision, letting their height speak.

The woman from Tallahassee wrote about her affairs. Living near her father who was Satan. Becoming adjusted to freedom. She was easy and friendly as if nothing had happened. However, I thought I detected a patronizing tone. She took me for a common fool, I decided. I drove to the home of my ex-woman. When she came out in the yard I promised her that in the future evil would come upon her. Or perhaps we could get married, I added.

At the end of a bender I have, like thousands of others, been stricken with righteousness. I wanted to have discussions with the naked dead but I could not dream them back. At the gate of an air force base near Columbus, Mississippi, I was thrown out by APs after certain demonstrations. I claimed to have friends on the base, imperative that they see me. I drove following a contrail in the sky to New Orleans, got out of my car dropping money, and was mugged before I could let out I was in the secret ground air force they had better stand wide for. The mugging did not make much of an impression on me. Unlike other drunks, I remember almost everything. Only the humiliation is left out, until later it leaps and is unbearable.

I turned toward Florida, seeking Tyndall air base beyond Panama City. I would have a chat with the pals there who didn't know me yet, perhaps even her ex-husband down on a mission, then on to Tallahassee where I would explain to the woman I was not a fool. No, I was in control, in vast control. But first I took a turn into Magnolia Springs on the eastern shore of Mobile Bay, where an old student of mine lived.

We talked a while. His parents were in the back, visiting, but he did not want me to meet them. Then he asked me to go, please. So I took my bottles and left in a huff. It seemed to me the world was certainly turning rude here lately, a lamentable sign of the times, those times you read about. Oh I was high into my righteousness, and just out near some swamp and palmettos I went way off into it and attempted to set fire to my car, which would not fly and was really hot on my feet. I threw matches into it, a '73 MG convertible. Then somebody stopped my arm. He put out the little rug fire I'd started. He was the son of a strange nearby family who fed me for three days. I could not decide whether they were white or colored.

They didn't pay much attention to me and did not speak much, but I thought I caught a foreign brogue, not creole, when they did. They ate rice and collards. This brought my health back in little angry fragments. One morning I was suddenly very sober, just very frail. They didn't mind how much I ate because they had their eye on my car over there out of sight. Then my old student came back and told me he was taking me home. I never gave them the car but I gave them the keys and was ashamed to return a week later. My student took a look around my cottage, then took a U-turn back the long trip. I still did not understand I had been gently but seriously kicked out of his county, 350 miles far.

My old girlfriend married the Texan. In the fall I got a call from my nephew who had heard from a musician that she was killed in a robbery of her bank in Jacksonville, Florida. Killed by crack people. She was no doubt in her smart executive suit, all bright and cheerful. New leaf, new man. She was not good with people, she once told me. Maybe a bit of a snob. I understand the new breed of crack killer is much concerned with respect. Something in her eyes, maybe. Maybe nothing at all, she was white and too lovely. She was there. I thought of her father, the dour banker on that hill in the east Texas town, her tiny thin mother. One of their daughters was a lesbian psychiatrist and the other was now dead from banking. He hustled peas in the Depression and now he was in modern life, on the hill there with the wind blowing the last of his hair.

Nevertheless, it is said we are predators, eyes forward, and we go on towards the hunt, as if nobody had eaten it all before us. As if just around the corner is the really fine feed, the really true woman, the world that will call us son. Somebody is missing to our left but we only sniff deeper, it must be there, there.

I was doing this in the aisle of a small local grocery when I turned a row and was shocked chilly, down to the bones of my hands, nearly crippled from a swat of cold nerves into my thighs and scalp. It was a very tall man all naked, in a large hat. He had a long gray country face I was certain I knew, a man confined somehwere too long.

The crown of the hat was above the top shelf of cans. He was turning my way to look but I did not want him to look at me. Then I noticed he was in a bleached pink set of long underwear, not naked, but the possibility was so close it was jolting. He opened his mouth. I ran away with my hands and groceries in my ears, with his lips twisting up there over me.

I went out in the street with the groceries still in my hands. Nobody called me back. I was well home before I was aware I had them, still locked in my fingers. I had no excuse for running out with them, for running away, noth-

ing manly anyway. My act could not be explained. I was ill
and ashamed, and jerking with breaths.

Next day I got a letter from the woman—now twenty-
five—in Tallahassee. My hands still shook a little and my
breathing came hard. I was without sleep because I didn't
want to dream.

She wrote that things were not going very well. She
lived with her mother, but Satan, her father, lived close by.
Not going well. Too close, this man. As if he could move
away but not very far. It felt like forever. It hurt to discuss
certain things.

She asked me to forgive *her*. She had visited me with
her winter pounds shed and with a dark suntan so as to hurt
me, in her vanity. To make my mouth water. But yet I was
her friend and this could no longer go unconfessed. She had
wanted to change and ruin me for a while, with her beauty.
It was an unfortunate trait. Her father had accused her of it
all her life, but only now she was truly adult could she admit
she enjoyed inflicting pain this way, always had. Her mother,
a beauty, was fast losing her looks and was always in a state,
afraid to go out with anybody new. She and her mother spent
the days simply keeping a watch on each other. They had
begun going to church together. Even there, they knew the
great Satan was in one of the cars in the parking lot, watching them.

You must never write about me, she wrote. *You think I
am special but I am not. I am to be forgotten, do you understand.
We have had a bad house, wherever I am is a bad room.*

A week later I won an award from the governor. My
old parents were there glowing in the mansion. I was in a
suit, now a goodly time healthy, but in my short acceptance
speech I was conscious of sneering ironic people somewhere
in the crowd. When I looked at the rear rank of those stand-

ing I did see three hats way above the rest and flashes of beige skin. I may have broken all forms for modesty, unwilled actually, but from a diminished heart, and held my work in an esteem equal to that of a scratching worm drowned in ink and flung against a tombstone. Through all this too I confess I was coming on to the governor's wife—helplessly, God—and finished in a burst of meekness coupled with hideous inappropriate lust. I could hear the laughter and was led away.

I was looking at the plaque and stroking myself a couple days later as the phone rang. A voice I could not remember began. At once I could feel the black wind of North Dakota between us on the lines. She was a friend of the Florida girl. I had not seen her since I chatted with them at that bar near the Minnesota line. She was clear for a while but then started sobbing and stalling. Her friend. Our friend. You were kind to her, she said. Always she mentioned your kindness. What?

In Tallahassee the father had run her over in her own living room and killed her. The car came in through the bay window and crushed her as she sat on the couch in her bikini swimsuit. Her mother, also in a swimsuit, was broken up badly but would survive. Abruptly after the collision, the father, still in the driver's seat, put a pistol to his ear and destroyed himself. The women were having lunch after sunning. He must have known all their moves. You are a good person, the woman said—a scrap of memory through the black air of days and days ago—and I had to tell a good person. Somebody who knew her.

I am not a good person, I told her. This is too awful.

Do you believe in God?

Foxhole Christian. When all else is lost.

Nothing else was said and she hung up.

I was suddenly something fresh to her, a way I did not know. Then she was destroyed by a monster I had never believed in, who was true. My pity was so confused I could not accept I was even worthy of having it, for weeks. Or worthy of her, or my former girlfriend.

It is true now that, years later and desperately married (to the daughter of a World War II pilot named Angel), whenever a flute plays I have the woman sweet in my ears and think of our laughter. Wherever I see a headline beauty I brag quietly: Come on, I had a better, with a sad smile, I'd imagine, that fine appreciation of ourselves when we have bittersweetness right on time.

I have not had that many women, is the truth, and this, pal, I know seems crammed with serial romance and grief, but I'm not quite through, and you will understand me at last as more that poor man on the east Texas hill with the wind in his last hairs, too thick in modern life, too thick in dream, too sad for years now. Maybe the girl in North Dakota mistook my sadness for kindness; defeat for gentleness. I look at an old photograph of myself at eight when I was just a boy and his dog under a cowboy hat. I was looking at the world across the cornfield, all ready to touch it all under the shade of my tall Hoot Gibson. Now I understand I have been witness to the worst fifty years in the history of the world. A tragedy that might make Caligula weep in commiseration. And I have had, you know, a relatively pampered life, although you see me puffing away on my smoke like a leathered vet, a tough cookie.

I used to be a considerable tennis player. So in my health I took it up again and got the game back quickly. I just had a tough time giving a damn about the score. Once I was playing with a friend and noticed a very tall pale woman

through the fence on another court. She had her back to me.
I saw she struck the ball with authority and grace. I wanted
her within seconds of seeing her. I needed her. I had never
had a tall woman, blond, and I was already in my mind rocking with her in great abandon like a dying cannibal. The
nourishment would be endless, so generous.

My friend and I played well. We sat down exhausted
in that fine chill of Southern twilight that heaven might be.
I looked to my right and somehow, in the flesh, the tall pale
woman was sitting between us. You never see that kind of
European paleness in women on a Southern tennis court. I
was amazed at her musculature, like strands of soft wire.
Then I saw the hat. She had been wearing a big unusual hat
that must have given her seven feet in height. She was looking toward my friend. I had never seen her face. When she
turned I looked away and in great fear I stared through the
woods. I wanted her more than ever but I would not see her
face. I heard her voice, though, just the once up close.

I believe I've got something you want.

I grabbed my bag and got in my car and was almost
home before I remembered my friend had no ride home, a
long way. But I couldn't go back and I almost threw up.

He called me, however.

Man, the woman was fast on you. What the devil,
did you *see* all of her, fool? I'm much the better-looking, but
all she gave me was a pouting ride home.

Who is she?

Somebody's relative. Can't remember. Too busy
stealing looks. That's quite a drink of water, long and cool,
old son. You never knew her?

Never set eyes on her.

You're an uncommon fool. And sober.

She has been around town now for a couple of years. I see parts of her here and there, but I walk or drive right away. I don't intend to see her face because I know I've already seen it. When we touch one of us will die and be in the other's dreams.

I am not insane. My affairs are composed in vicious sobriety. I did not see my tennis partner either for several months. Then he called at the end of the summer.

You don't play anymore?

A few times, other places.

The tall one was back on the courts the other day. I swear, fool, she's like something from the heart of winter in a foreign land. Same old story full of wolves where you'd stumble into a woman lying in the woods. I'm going to use a word. *Alabaster.*

I swallowed. You mean living or dead?

I'm not sure, mister.

Wolves.

I wonder, when she dies, likely by violence, will she be named like the lesser creatures in that story? Certain people believe all are given names when we die, not at birth.

The creature goes to heaven very baffled.

My God, what was all that about? it asks.

God says: Well, you were a wolf.

I see, says the wolf.

I wonder will it be that simple for her, or for me.

The Ice Storm

MOST OF THE LEAVES ARE FALLEN AND THIS PLACE LOOKS bombed all over again. Last February the ice storm of the century passed through the Arkansas delta into north Mississippi and lower Tennessee up to Nashville. Eleven at night, I was out in the front yard waiting for it, led by a special alarm, even horror, in the voice of the television weathercaster. Like a Jeremiah just miles ahead of the storm and pointing backwards down the road, raving. The edge of the storm came on in feather-light little BB's, then began to drive and pile. The glass on the west of the house went pecking as if attacked by a gale of birds. Under the streetlights the swirls of white-silver turned almost opaque. It was a determined blizzard. A Southerner doesn't see such driving ice more than twice in a lifetime. But at one I went to bed pleasantly aroused, rich as a caveman with the weather outside.

When my wife and I awoke, civilization as we knew it had mainly shut down. Luckily we had gas heaters. All electricity and water were gone; no telephone, all local radio stations kaput. Outside, the trees were draped sculptures in white, but in their quietness, a whole new storm of ghouls.

I am an addict of great weathers. Had I been in Hurricane Camille, which struck the Mississippi coast in 1969, I would be dead. I would have been the leading fool in some motel party hoisting a silver mug, crying havoc, hailing and adoring the wind until blasted off like a kite. Twelve years ago I decided I wanted Oxford for my home when I was having coffee at the Hoka, a café in a warehouse with a tin roof. A violent rainstorm came up. The sound of it thrash-

187

ing on the tin moved something deep within me, a memory of another storm, my pals and me in a barn sleeping on hay when I was a boy: That tin roof was the margin against everything dangerous.

But at noon when limbs and then whole trees began falling around me, nothing was nice. The picturesque had turned into terror. Whatever we were, whatever good and rotten had transpired in this, our little jewel of a city, these trees had witnessed it. Now they were splitting apart and falling wholesale with mournful cracks and awful thuds. They were coming in the window glass like dead uncles. Next door, an eighty-foot tree fell on a neighbor woman's Mercedes, the fetish of her life. She came out into the driveway wailing as I've never heard a white person wail. But you see a whole tree go over like that, and your grip on the universe goes. A small mob of slackers came down the block and stood around the big tree over the Mercedes. They grinned, sort of worshiping the event. But the woods running down a hill to the east went into an exploding mutual collapse too much like the end of the world, and everyone fled back inside.

All these old trees were like family in the act of dying; their agony was more terrible than the storm itself. We had been confident, even arrogant, with them around us, I realized. They'd been comforting brothers and sisters. Now the town was suddenly half as tall.

In the next weeks, trucks and electricians from four states poured into town. You would drive around very stupidly and like a zombie point to another great oak down, another smashed roof: Look at that, Sue. A vast pile of debris burned like the end of a war out on the west edge of town.

You hear a fatuous volume about growing, nurturing, and blossoming as a person nowadays. But great subtractions must be granted too. There is not always more of us, growing, flapping leaves around like idiot vines.

Here under a rare storm of ice we got our come-uppance. The leaves are gone, and we see it all over again. Lessness rules.

In the spring, I saw a histrionic young woman, the daughter of a highway patrolman, who had starred in one of Hood's cheap movies. She was on her way to San Francisco. Enough of small-town life. I asked if she'd seen Hood. He hadn't been on the courts this season. He was a decent player with a nice chopped approach shot. Hood too was Nordic and barely had an expression when he played. Once somebody asked me who was that frozen Swede I'd just played. But he had certain aggressions about his work and attended workshops for playwrights all over the country.

You didn't hear? asked Shannon.

Hood had been in California during the earthquake last January. His apartment was all thrown around. For a while he tried to hang on in Los Angeles, but his nerves kept getting to him, so he moved back here to exercise his art on firm land. A generator came with his house, out a bit from town, and he was whistling about his luck after the ice storm, because most had no water and there were long lines of country and town folks down at the ice house, which had a natural spring under it. Hood was whistling in his shower, all loose in an orgy of steam, when an oak tree about the age of the Civil War fell down through the roof into the shower and broke his leg. He lay in his house for two days, phones out, until a neighbor's dog came through the broken wall and the neighbor right after it. By then Hood was hoarse from screaming. His body, not just the leg, was poisoned green, black, and yellow.

In the fall, though, I saw him at the courts with another chum, and he seemed to be moving all right. Somebody had printed up T-shirts about the ice storm of '94 and I was wearing one. Hood was not amused. We did play one night, but after just a few games he called it off. There was a real whine in his voice and a difference in his eyes. I had been serving very well, but my serve hadn't frightened anybody since I was thirty. He didn't say much, yet I heard another whine and this: "I can't, I just can't." He got in his Jeep and pulled away, fretting. I'd liked Hood's peculiarity. It was a shame to see him wussed.

I bought a video camera, my first, because I felt like life was getting away from me and wanted to shoot scenes of my wife naked or nearly so in compromising positions. I know this is the act of an aging creep who cannot understand his good luck, but I had ceased to care. I paid a great deal for this thing but what I could not buy was any desire to use it once it was in my hands. The first time I raised it I felt like an idiot and my wife ran away raving into the backyard. I just toiled there, whispering about my tender aims. Maybe I was in Hood's world, a deeply wretched place.

I visited my mother a good deal that last year of her life. I did not know she was in the act of dying, wracked by the worst arthritis. But I worked close by her so we could chat occasionally. I was on the back glassed porch to keep the cigarette smoke away from her. I was working very well, almost under a miracle burst.

We had got very honest with each other. The old black lady who spent the nights with her had seen the white horse of death in the sky after a recent funeral. We talked about this, Mother and I, and she told me the old woman had introduced herself by saying "Ma'am, I ain't not rogue." This was finally understood as *thief*. She was a true old-timey woman although a bit younger than my mother, in her early eighties. Each day now I watched the diminishing of my mother. She was tiny, that woman who had controlled so much.

I thought of Hood, just to speak of something.

In another playwrighting workshop at the university he had become an out-and-out bitch who led insurrections against the teacher. He never spoke in class but wrote notes of delicious scorn. The teacher knew nothing, nothing. The lively girls who had been in Hood's movies avoided him, but Hood was unaware of this. The distance in his eyes was shortened. His art vision was gone, replaced by much sighing and staring at the floor.

A great Nordic *bitch*, I finished.

"Please don't use that word," my mother said, "What could it possibly mean in relation to a young man?"

"Well, the tree might have done him in."

"That's not a man, then, son. He would be grateful he survived, happy in his health, not angry he was hurt. Believe: Your mother knows whereof she speaks."

Still, the biggest oak anywhere right through the shower.

Then we talked about the Mississippi flood of 1927. She was there, in Leland, about to leave for college. She was in it, child. Broken levees, bodies, rain and ruin. My poor daddy, responsible to everybody on the plantation. You can't tell me.

Where I work men spent several months putting in a criss-cross graded walk for the handicapped in wheelchairs. It had blue iron rails and resting benches, very stylish. The thing was superior to the ordinary walks by far.

One afternoon I noticed a man in a cape and a beret rolling down in a chair. Across the arms, too, he held a cane.

This was a lot of costume for early fall or I'd not have noticed. Under the beret was a long blond face, very surly. It was Hood. Before I knew this, I'd had in mind one of the great wounded artists of the fin de siècle. He was enrolled in yet another workshop.

But I have it on witness by his last vixen, a nurse, that, in truth, there is nothing wrong with him.

Drummer Down

HE HAD NEVER LIKED THE YOUNG DANCING ASTAIRE, ALL GREEDY and certain. But now he was watching an old ghost thriller, and he liked Astaire old, pasted against the wall of mortality—dry, scared, maybe faintly alcoholic. This was a man. He pitied him. Everything good had pity in it, it seemed to Smith, now fifty and a man of some modest fashion himself. Even as a drunkard he had been a bit of a dandy. It was midnight when he turned off the set. He had begun thinking sadly about his friend Drum again, the man whose clothes were a crying shame. Drum two summers ago had exchanged his .22 for a pistol of a large bore, one that was efficient. In his bathtub in a trailer home on the outskirts of that large town in Alabama, he had put the barrel in his mouth. He had counted off the days on his calendar a full month ahead of the event of his suicide, and on the date of it he had written "Bye Bye Drum." The note he left was not original. It was a vile poem off the bathroom wall, vintage World War II. He had destroyed his unpublished manuscripts and given away all his other art and had otherwise put his affairs in order, with directions he was to be cremated and there was to be no ceremony.

But two young friends had organized a ceremony for themselves. Many had loved and needed Drum. They had pleaded over the phone for Smith, of all people, to gather with them, but the town was such a valley of the shadow to Smith, with an air choked by rotten cherries and whiskey, he did not go. He felt cowardly and selfish, because it was ceremonies of pity that most moved him now, but he could not take his part. He asked his sons to appear at the ceremony for him. They wore suits and went to the funeral home and stood with a mournful group of people in wretched cheap dark clothes, and stood quietly for an hour before they discovered it was a rite for another person.

Smith did not like arithmetic or its portents, but he recalled Drum at his death was sixty-six, twice the age of Christ at Golgotha. With Drum this was relevant, and overbore the vile poem. Drum had been a successful carpenter several years previous.

But in Smith's class ten years before the end, Drum was fifty-six and looked much like Charles Bronson. Big flat nose and thin eyes with a blue nickel gleam in them; three marriages behind him, and two sons by an opera singer far away in Germany. He held a degree in aeronautical engineering from UCLA. He could fix anything, and with stern joyful passion. He had written six unpublished novels. He served in the army in Panama in the years just after the world war, which he would have been a bit young for. Smith stole glances at Drum while he taught, or tried to, with his marriage and grip on things going to pieces. He tried to understand why this old man was in his class, whether he was a fool or a genius. There were indications both ways.

As in Smith's progress toward the condition of a common drunkard.

Smith wanted to be both lost and found, an impossibility. He was nearly begging to be insane. He saw this fellow of great persuasive ugliness, with his small airy voice and his sighs; the weariness about him, even with his blocky good build and the forearms of a carpenter. He was popular in class even these short weeks into the semester. Drummond was his last name. He pleased the girls around him. He was avuncular and selfless in his comments, with a beam of patient affection in his eyes. Somehow he scared Smith, Drum holding his smile, the flattened great bags under his eyes from rough living and failure. He spoke often of "love" and "quest." He prefaced many things he said with "I am a Christian," sadly, as if he were in some dreadful losers' club.

Paul Smith looked at the table in front of him and had a brief collapse.

"I'm sorry." He put his hands down flat. There seemed to be a whole bleak country in front of his eyes, the ten hills of his fingers on the desert floor of linoleum, speckled by gray lakes, all dry. "I'm sorry to be confusing. Things aren't going well at home. Bear with me."

Drum befriended him. He seemed to be just all at once there, his hand on Smith's shoulder and the grave twinkle in his eyes. The little smile of a prophet on his lips. Two of the very attractive girls from the class, right behind him, were looking concerned. Maybe they liked Smith. He didn't know. He couldn't get a read on much at all these days. Arrogance punctuated by bouts of heartbreaking sentiment had come on Smith since the publication of his last book, which was hailed by major critics and bought by a few hundred people.

He didn't want to be arrogant, but he was experiencing a gathering distaste for almost everybody. He would nowadays mumble and shout a few things in anguish that seemed loud and eternal, then call class. To others that might seem derelict, but many of his students grandly appreciated the quick hits and release, right in the manner of a punk lecture. Punk was all the rage that year, and in his class was a lame girl wearing a long sash with sleigh bells on it, so that when she wallowed along in the hall on big stomping crutches, a holy riot ensued. She wore enormous eyeglasses but was otherwise dressed and cut punk, wearing a hedge of waxed hair atop her tubular head. She was the punkest of them all, a movement unto herself. Smith noticed that Drum was very kind to her and cheered her various getups every class meeting. The girl was unceasingly profane too. This seemed to interest Drum even more. He grinned and applauded her, this funny Christian Drum.

Nevertheless, she had gone to the chairwoman about Smith's asthmatic style. She loved his hungover explosions, but complained that he cut them too short and she was not getting her money's worth. Smith was incredulous. It was his first experience with a vocal minority, the angry disabled woman. Angel B. was very serious about her writing—very bad—and viewed it as her only salvation. He was not imparting the secrets of the art to her. She must know everything, no holding back. All this with a punk's greediness and nearly solid blue language, the bells shaking. Smith noted that he made no complaint about the bells. Smith planned to kill her and insist on one of her prettier banalities for her headstone, so that she could be mocked for centuries. But this man Drum loved her even as the talentless bitch she was. How could he be here offering to help Smith?

"What can we do, Paul?" Drum was whispering and uncle-ish. The two girls nodded their wishes to help too. Smith looked them over. He was already half in love with the taller one, pretty with lean shanks, who looked like she was right then slipping into a bathtub with Nietzsche, that lovely caution about her. The other was pre-Raphaelite, a mass of curly hair around a pale face very oval, the hair coiled up on her cheeks and separating for the full lips.

"We could drink," said Smith, dying for a taste. He was imagining a long telescope of whiskey and soda through which to view these newcomers to his pain. He liked people waving like liquid images, hands reaching toward him.

At home the end was near. His wife, just out of the tub, would cover her breasts with her arms as she went to her drawers in their bedroom. Smith watched, alarmed and in grief. No old times anymore. She meant, These are for something else, somewhere else down the road. He had hoped to hang on to ambivalence just a little bit longer. He wanted her more than ever. He said unforgettable, brutal things to her. His mouth seemed to have its own rude life. Here he was, no closer to her than a ghoul gazing through a knothole to her toilet, the hole rimmed with slobber, in their own big smart house.

They all went to the Romeo Bar on the university strip. Smith saw Drum drive up with the girls in a bleached mustard Toyota with a bee drawn on it at the factory. Smith thought it was an art statement, but it was not. Drum was poor.

He wore unironed clothes, things deeply cheap, dead and lumpy even off the rack at bargain barns, and the color of harmful chemicals, underneath them sneakers with Velcro snaps instead of shoestrings. The clothes of folks from a broken mobile home, as a pal of Smith's had described them. Drum at fifty-six lived upstairs in a small frame house of asbestos siding. In the lower story lived his mother, whom he called the Cobra. The brand of his smokes was Filter Cigarettes. His beer was white cans labeled Beer.

Nothing surprised Drum, and the girls were rapt as Smith poured forth. He was a bothered half-man, worn out by the loss of heart and music of the soul.

Drum agreed about the times, entirely. "There should be only a radio in every home, issuing bulletins on the war. The war of good against evil. That's all the news we need," he said, directing the bar air like a maestro. "But all they give us is facts, numbers, times. Enough of this and nobody cares about the war anymore. Why, all television addresses is the busybody in everybody!

"We're born to kill each other. First thing in the morning we take something to numb us, then parachute into the sordid zones of reality. Layers of dead skin on us, layers!" he finished.

Everything surprised the girls. They seemed to adore being confidantes in Drum's presence. They were anxious to become writers and have sorrows of their own. The grave male details of Smith's distress the girls thought exquisite. That through a knothole looking at her toilet thing was beautiful, said the pre-Raphaelite Minny.

Later, they all stayed over at Smith's green hovel by the railroad tracks he'd rented as his writing place, a heart-breaking first move toward divorce. Minny took ether and began talking about her enormous clitoris, a thing that kept her in nerves and panic every waking hour. Pepper passed out before she could recall any true sorrow. Drum went back in the kitchen with some of Smith's stories. He had on half-glasses bought at a drugstore, and Smith saw him foggily as a god: Charles Bronson as a kitchen god. Smith retired with Minny.

Then in the morning his wife knocked on the door. Smith answered in a leather overcoat, nude underneath. He was stunned by drink and ether, and his wife's presence simply put a sharpness on his wrecked eyesight. Behind him in a bedsheet sat Minny in front of a drum set. She was sitting there smiling at Smith's palomino-haired wife. It was her first scandal, she told them later.

His wife said something about divorce papers, and Smith slapped her. She rammed the door shut.

"Oh, how Old World!" Minny cried. She dropped the sheet and rose naked and curly like something from a fountain. Already Smith was tired of her. He loved Pepper, the lean beauty who could not get her sorrow out, asleep in the rear room.

"That's no good, Paul. You shouldn't hit" Drum had awoken and come out. His big fingers were around a fresh cold beer. "Oh, I hit my second wife. She thrived on it. Some women like hitting, they work for it. But it's a bad thing. A man of your sensitivity, with that sad little child in you, *you* won't survive, is what I'm saying."

"I love the sad child!" said Minny.

"But it makes an end to things at least. You need to end things, Paul. Purgatory is much rougher than hell. Well I know. You've got to wish them well, and be off. Wish them well in love, hope they have good orgasms."

"My God!" Smith could not imagine this charity.

Sometime later in the week Smith asked Drum how he'd lost three wives.

"Because I was a failure, man!" Drum seemed delighted. "I wrote and wrote and couldn't get published. I quit all my jobs. I'd had it with facts, the aeronautics industry. Working plans to fly in a *coal mine,* baby! The heart, Paul, the heart, that's where it is."

On the last of his GI bill the man was taking ceramics, photography, sculpture, and Smith's writing class.

"I *pride* myself on being a dilettante! I am looking for accidental successes. Heart accidents. I want to slip down and fall into something wonderful!"

As for Drum's physical heart, there was a bad thing running in his family. His father and two older brothers had gone out early with coronaries, and he himself took nitroglycerin tablets to ward off angina.

Even Smith's punk band excited Drum. Anything declamatory of the heart moved him. He was very often their only audience. He applauded and commended, through their vileness. They switched instruments, versatile in absence of talent. It didn't matter.

"*Everything* must be explored! Nothing left untouched!" Drum shouted, slugging down his cheap beer, smoking his generics.

They played their own "Yeast Infection Blues" and a filthy cover of George Jones's "He Stopped Loving Her Today." The regular guitarist was a vicious harelip pursued all over town for bad checks. The singer was a round man with dense eyeglasses and a squint who sold term papers to fraternity boys. They called him the Reverend. The bassman was a boy who never wore shoes, hardly bathed, and in appearance approached the late Confederate veterans around Appomattox—gaunt, hang-necked, and smutty. Drum absorbed them all. They were his children, junior alcoholics to Smith. Sometimes he'd dance with Minny or Pepper. They shook the little green house and the police came. Perfect.

Smith poured Southern Comfort in a Pepsi can in order to make it through his lectures, which seemed a crucifixion. The crippled girl Angel B. seemed satisfied, liberated more thoroughly and writing even worse. As for his own heart, Smith wanted to get rid of it. He missed his wife terribly. The thing pounded as if it were an enormous fish in him. He was barred from his old home. The band was angry over his lack of endurance on the drums. One night Drum brought him over some chicken soup, vitamin B, and gluconate. He was worried.

"Look at you. Look at this room," he said.

Smith's SS overcoat was spattered with white paint. He had painted everything instead of cleaning. He had painted even Minny's dog. It was under the table licking itself. He had nailed bedsheets to the floor. The novel he was writing was strewn out in copies all over the musical instruments. He and the band were singing his novel. The children from his first marriage were not allowed to visit him anymore. He had been fired at the college. Bare inside his overcoat, with a Maltese cross made by Drum hanging from a chain around his neck, he had grown so thin that his wedding band had fallen off somewhere. He was now almost pure spirit, as Minny called him.

"We need your big heart, Paul. The forces of good need you. Technique and facts and indifference are out there winning. Money is winning, mere form and the tightasses are winning. Commerce is making the town uglier and uglier. We Christians need you. You're giving over to low anger and spite, drinking away your talent. An old bad thing coiled in the dust, that's not you."

Smith poured the remainder of a jar of cherries into a mug half filled with Southern Comfort. The overcoming taste would remind Smith forever of his last days in this town.

Drum had made the mug. On it was an ugly face with a cigarette in its lip. It was one of the forms of "Sarge," an old army drunk Drum had known in Panama. The man had been only in his thirties, like Smith, but already grotesque. He would line up for review every morning, everything wrong with his uniform, but with a tiny smile and ruined goggle-eyes, maimed in every inch by the night before. He'd been busted from sergeant four times.

Later Smith fought with the band and threw them out. Minny ran out of Valium. Now living was almost impossible without constant fornication. People with police records began showing up in the house. Some played musical instruments or sang, then stole the equipment. One night while he was plying Minny, who poured out high spiritual sighs, he had to have a drink. On his way to the kitchen, he caught a thief in the house. The man sprinted out the back window as Smith pulled his father's antique shotgun off the wall. Then out came Minny, screaming for him please to not shoot anybody.

In the morning he accused her and her dog, who had remained silent, of setting him up. He put the cur in her arms and kicked them both out. Then he fell out in a sleep of a few hours. When he woke up it was midafternoon, and he knew something was gone. The antique shotgun was not on the wall. He stumbled to his kitchen and pulled a hunting knife out of his drawer. He intended to cut Minny's pre-Raphaelite hair off and drag her down the railroad tracks by her ankles. In a swimsuit and his serious coat he went out to the tracks. He seemed to remember her other place was near the tracks somewhere down there. So he walked and walked and then he was in a black section of town, there in his overcoat with lion-tamer boots on, holding the large saw of his knife, in the hottest summer on record. In the overcoat he was drenched, just an arm with the pounding awful fish of his heart inside him. A black teenager, tall, came out of one of the houses and asked him what he was doing with that knife out here, his mama didn't like it.

"Hunting woman."

"You sit down in that tree shade." Smith gave him the knife. "How much you take for that coat? I can get that paint off it."

"I'll sell you the coat if you'll call a number for me. I don't feel good. I'm not all right. Here's some money. Please get me some liquor too." He gave his wallet to the boy.

"You wait."

When Drum at last came out across the tracks and knelt beside him, Smith had terrible shakes, and could not pass out like he wanted to.

"You think you're drunk, kiddo? Shit, this is nothing. I was drunker. And I was drunker *alone*." Drum laughed.

Smith sold the black boy his coat for fifty dollars and got back his wallet. Then Smith stared into his wallet.

"Drum? I got exactly the same in my wallet. That boy bought my coat with my own money."

"Forget it. It was a horrible coat. A chump's coat. A pretender's coat. It was the coat of a man with a small dry heart."

"It was?"

Smith was out of money now, but he was waiting for a *Reader's Digest* sweepstakes check very seriously. His unopened mail was a foot high, but none of it was the right envelope. Then a letter came offering him some work in Hollywood. He took it around town, running up tabs with credit on it. Some people still liked Smith. One night late he came in from drinking and misplacing his car. He felt there was something new in the place. Yes, there it was. On the kitchen table. The kitchen had been cleaned. But on the table was the final version of "Sarge," the life-size ceramic head of the grinning old drunk, the butt of a real Pall Mall hanging from his lips. Drum, a year in labor on it, had given it to Paul Smith. There was a short note underneath it: "All yours. Go with Sarge." Smith did not know it then, but this was as far as Drum would ever go in the arts. At first it made Smith afraid. He thought it was an insult. But then he knew it wasn't. He laid his head down and wept. He had lost everything. He did not deserve this friend.

About three in the morning, into the last of his cheap wine, he heard a car in his drive and some bells at his door. It was Angel B., the punk crippled girl. She settled inside with her crutches and her bells on what was left of a wicker armchair.

"I know I can't write, but you are a great man. I can get your job back for you. I know some things on the person fired you, some of them taped. This would destroy her."

It seemed a plausible and satisfactory thing to Smith.

"I might not can write but I want a piece of a great man to remember. Would you dim the lights?"

He recalled the revulsion, but with an enormous pity overcoming it. In his final despair, the last anguished thrust and hold, he tried to mean actual love. He wanted to be a heavy soft trophy to her. The bells jangled faintly every now and then before he accomplished the end of his dream. Smith stroked Angel's mohawk, grown high and soft. Then she was businesslike getting her clothes and crutches back together. She was leaving immediately. Smith suggested they at least have a wine together.

"No. I'm drinking with Morris, the Reverend. He's out there waiting. We've got a tough morning tomorrow. We're going down to the station and I'm putting rape charges on him."

"He's driving you? What, pleading guilty?"

"No, innocent. We're still close. But I know what I know."

She waddled out to the old Mustang. Morris waited in it like a pet. His dense glasses were full of moonlight.

A week later Drum drove him to the airport.

"I think that was it, Drummer. Pit bottom. And I can still taste her." Smith was trying to get a long march out of sips of Southern Comfort.

"It probably wasn't, sport. You get to go to California, stomping grounds of all *my* failures. Be patient, Paul. Nobody gets well quick, not with what you've got."

He remembered Drum taking his luggage. The man wore a shapeless blue-green jumpsuit with plastic sandals on his feet. The porter was a diplomat, compared.

Smith was not a success as a screenwriter. After he destroyed two typewriters, he spent a month in a hospital, where they talked about the same little child inside that Drum had often mentioned. Smith was befriended by a kind genius of a director, one of his heroes. The man gave him money that put him right with his child support, but Smith was unable to compose anything worthy for him, for all his effort. The bright healthy weather and opulence mocked him. He could not get past stupid good feelings. His work was entirely made up and false. There was no saving it by pure language. He could not work sober and was greatly frightened by this fact. He was failing right along with the old Drummer. He had to take another teaching job in the Midwest. It was a prestigious place, but Smith felt dumb and small.

He kept up with Drum through the years left. The Drummer was making a lot of money as a carpenter in house construction. He wrote to Smith that he could have, if he were not a Christian, any number of miserable lonely housewives. The Cobra, his quarrelsome mother, died. He moved out to a big mobile home on the outskirts of town, near Cottondale. He attended the high school graduation of Smith's son. He took and sent over a photograph of the boy in his gown receiving his diploma. He gave Smith's children presents at Christmas. Many times he took them fishing.

Three years ago, Smith had bitten the bullet and visited Drum in his trailer. Drum had had a heart attack six months previous. He told Smith he could hold in pain, but this was too much. He drove himself to the hospital. Uninsured, he paid out a ghastly amount. The trailer was all he could afford now. A preacher had become his landlord. Smith offered to lend him some money. Drum refused.

"Oh no. We don't want money to get into this, baby. Somehow things go rotten with money between friends. Believe me. This thing we have is too beautiful."

The streets of the town were a long heart attack themselves to Smith. Everything felt like sorrow and confusion, and tasted like Southern Comfort with cherry juice poured in—a revulsion of the tongue that had never left him. He felt the town itself was mean and fatal, each street a channel of stunned horror. He feared for Drum's health. How could he carry on here?

He met Drum's woman, a handsome lady of Greek descent. Drum was wild for her. She stayed over the night in their larger bedroom at the other end of the trailer. When she left, Smith told Drum he was very happy for him.

"I worried you'd turned queer," Smith kidded him.

"You ought to hear her moan, boy. I'm bringing happiness to that one."

Now Smith saddened, and his teeth cut into his tight underlip. Drum all those years without a woman, the uncle to everybody, in the background, cheering them on; urging them on to the great accidents of art and love. Drum the Drummer. Keeping the panic out, keeping the big heart in. He had convinced Smith he was worth something. He had convinced others that Smith was rare. Many days in California Smith had nothing else to take him through the blank stupid days.

"I'm living on borrowed time, man. Nothing is unimportant. Every minute is a jewel. Every stroke of pussy, every nail in the board."

He had lived that way every minute Smith had known him. That seemed very clear now. He looked at his friend and a shock passed through him. Drum was old, with wisps of gray hair combed back. He was pale, his eyes wet. The strong arms gestured and the mouth moved, but Smith heard nothing. Then the voice, like a whisper almost, came back. What was he saying? The vision had overcome everything.

It occurred to Smith later that success did not interest Drum. When Smith told him of some publishing luck and gave him a book, the man just nodded. You could see the boredom, almost distaste, freeze his eyes. He was not jealous. It simply didn't matter.

Near the end he had broken off relations with the Greek woman. His oldest son had come back from Germany to live with him, but he could not live with anybody. He asked him to leave the trailer.

And then the poem when they found him:

> *Here I sit all brokenhearted.*
> *Paid a nickel to shit,*
> *And only farted.*

A common piece of trash off a bathroom wall, a punkish anonymity.

How could he? Why not even a try at high personal salute? The way he had believed in work, the big heart, the war.

Smith was angry a long time that Drum had left nothing else.

The waiting on borrowed time, the misery of his heart yearning like a bomb, the bad starving blood going through his veins. Smith could understand the suicide. Who was good for endless lingering, a permanent bad seat and bad magazine at the doctor's office? And with heaven looming right over there, right next to you salvation and peace, what Christian could hold out any longer?

Yes, but the poem.

So common, so punk, so lost in democracy, like an old condom.

The wretched clothes, beneath and beyond style, the style of everybody waiting intolerable lengths of time in an emergency room. Clothes the head of Sarge belonged on, the smile of ruin on his lips. Here, sir. All accounted for.

Uncle High Lonesome

THEY WERE COMING TOWARD ME—THIS WAS 1949—ON THEIR horses with their guns, dressed in leather and wool and canvas and with different sporting hats, my father and his brothers, led by my uncle on these his hunting lands, several hundred acres called Tanglewood still dense in hardwoods but also opened by many meadows, as a young boy would imagine from cavalry movies. The meadows were thick with fall cornstalks, and the quail and doves were plenty. So were the squirrels in the woods where I had been let off to hunt at a stand with a Thermos of chocolate and my 28-gauge double. At nine years old I felt very worthy for a change, even though I was a bad hunter.

But something had gone wrong. My father had put me down in a place they were hunting toward. Their guns were coming my way. Between me and them I knew there were several coveys of quail to ground, frozen in front of the dogs, two setters and a pointer, who were now all stiffening into the point. My uncle came up first. This was my namesake, Peter Howard, married but childless at forty-five. I was not much concerned. I'd seen, on another hunt, the black men who stalked for my uncle flatten to the ground during the shooting, it was no big thing. In fact I was excited to be receiving fire, real gunfire, behind my tree. We had played this against Germans and Japanese back home in my neighborhood. But now I would be a veteran. Nobody could touch me at war.

My uncle came up alone on his horse while the others were still hacking through the overhang behind him. He was quite a picture. On a big red horse, he wore a yellow plaid corduroy vest with watch chain across, over a blue broadcloth shirt. On his bald head was a smoky brown fedora. He propped up an engraved 16-gauge double in his left hand and bridled with his right, caressing the horse with his thighs, over polo boots a high-gloss tan. An unlit pipe was fixed between his teeth. There was no doubting the man had a sort of savage grace, though I noticed later in the decade remaining to his life that he could also look, with his ears out, a bit common, like a Russian in the gate of the last Cold War mob; thick in the shoulders and stocky with a belligerence like Kruschev's. Maybe peasant nobility is what they were, my people. Uncle Peter Howard watched the dogs with a pleasant smile now, with the sun on his face at midmorning. I had a long vision of him. He seemed, there on the horse, patient and generous with his time and his lands, waiting to flush the quail for his brothers. I saw him as a permanent idea, always handy to reverie: the man who could do things.

In the face he looked much like—I found out later—the criminal writer Jean Genet, merry and Byzantine in the darks of his eyes. Shorter and stockier than the others and bald, like none of them, he loved to gamble. When he was dead I discovered that he also was a killer and not a valiant one. Of the brothers he was the most successful and the darkest. The distinct rings under my eyes in middle age came directly from him, and God knows too my religious acquaintance with whiskey.

The others, together, came up on their horses, ready at the gun. They were a handsome clan. I was happy to see them approach this way, champion enemy cavalry, gun barrels toward me, a vantage not many children in their protected childhoods would be privileged to have. I knew I was watching something rare, seen as God saw it, and I was warm in my ears, almost flushed. My uncle Peter tossed a stick over into a stalk pile and the quail came out with that fearsome helicopter bluttering always bigger than you are prepared for. The guns tore the air. You could see sound waves and feathers in a space of dense blue-gray smoke. I'd got behind my big tree. The shot ripped through all the leaves around. This I adored.

Then I stepped out into the clearing, walked toward the horses, and said hello.

My uncle Peter saw me first, and he blanched in reaction to my presence in the shooting zone. He nearly fell from his horse, like a man visited by a spirit-ghoul. He waddled over on his glossy boots and knelt in front of me, holding my shoulders.

"Boy? Boy? Where'd you come from? You were *there?*"

"Pete, son?" called my father, climbing down mystified. "Why didn't you call out? You could've, we could've. . . ."

My uncle hugged me to him urgently, but I couldn't see the great concern. The tree I was behind was wide and thick; I was a hunter, not a fool. But my uncle was badly shaken, and he began taking it out on my father. Maybe he was trembling, I guess now, from having almost shot yet another person.

"Couldn't you keep up with where your own boy was?"

"I couldn't know we'd hunt this far. I've seen you lost yourself out here."

An older cousin of mine had had his calf partially blown away in a hunting accident years ago, out squirrel hunting with his brother. Even the hint of danger would bring their wives to their throats. Also, I personally had had a rough time near death, though I hadn't counted up. My brother had nearly cut my head off with a sling blade when I walked up behind as a toddler, but a scar on the chin was all I had. A car had run me down as I crossed the street in first grade. Teaching me to swim the old way, my pa had watched me drown, almost, in the ocean off a pier he'd thrown me.

But this skit I had planned, it was no trouble. I wanted them to fire my way, and it had been a satisfactory experience, being in the zone of fire.

I felt for my father, who was I suppose a good enough man. But he was a bumbler, an infant at a number of tasks, although he was a stellar salesman. He had no grace, even though nicely dressed and handsome, black hair straight back, with always a good car and a far traveler in it around the United States, Mexico, and Canada. His real profession was a lifetime courting in awe of the North American continent—its people, its birds, animals, and fish. I've never met such a humble pilgrim of his own country as my father, who had the reverence of a Whitman and Sandburg together without having read either of the gentlemen. But a father's humility did not cut much ice with this son, although I enjoyed all the trips with him and Mother.

From that day on my uncle took more regard of me. He took me up, really, as his own, and it annoyed my turkey-throated aunt when I visited, which was often. We lived only an hour and a half away, and my uncle might call me up just to hear a baseball game on the radio with him as he drove his truck around the plantation one afternoon. On this vast place were all his skills and loves, and they all made money: a creosote post factory, turkey and chicken houses, cattle, a Big Dutchman farm machinery dealership; his black help in their gray weathered wrinkled houses; his lakes full of bass, crappie, bluegills, catfish, ducks and geese, where happy customer/friends from about the county were let fish and sport, in the spirit of constant merry obligation each to each that runs the rural South. Also there was a bevy of kin forever swarming toward the goodies, till you felt almost endlessly redundant in ugly distant cousins. Uncle Peter had a scratchy well-deep voice in which he offered free advice to almost everybody except his wife. And he would demand a hug with it and be on you with those black grinding whiskered cheeks before you could grab the truck door. He was big and clumsy with love, and over all a bit imperial; short like Napoleon, he did a hell of a lot of just . . . surveying. Stopping the truck and eyeballing what he owned as if it were a new army at rest across the way now, then with just the flick of his hand he'd . . . turn up the radio for the St. Louis Cardinals, the South's team then because the only broadcast around. I loved his high chesty grunts when one of his favorites would homer. He'd grip the steering wheel and howl in reverential delight: "Musial! Stan the Man!" I was no fan, a baseball dolt, but I got into it with my uncle.

Had I known the whole truth of where he had come from, I would have been even more impressed by his height and width of plenty. I mean not only from the degrading grunting Depression, beneath broke, but before that to what must have been the most evil hangover there is, in a jail cell with no nightmare but the actual murder of a human being in your mind, the marks of the chair legs he ground in your face all over you, and the crashing truth of your sorriness in gambling and drink so loud in your head they might be practicing the trapdoor for the noose over and over right outside the door. That night. From there. Before the family got to the jurors. Before the circuit judge showed up to agree that the victim was an unknown quantity from *out of town.* Before they convicted the victim of not being from here.

Before Peter himself might have agreed on his own reasonable innocence and smiled into a faint light of the dawn, just a little rent down on any future at all. That was a far trip, and he must have enjoyed it all every time we stopped and he, like Napoleon, surveyed.

He taught me to fish, to hunt, to handle dogs, and horses, to feed poultry. Then, one day, to stand watch at the post factory over a grown black man while he left in a truck for two hours. But this I highly resented.

"I want to see if this nigger can count. You tell me," he said, right in front of the man, who was stacking posts from the vat with no expression at all. He had heard but he didn't look at me yet, and I was afraid of when he would.

Such were the times that Peter Howard was hardly unusual in his treatment of black help around the farm. He healed their rifts, brought the men cartons of cigarettes. He got them medical treatment and extended credit even to children who had run away to Chicago. Sometimes he would sock a man in the jaw. I don't believe the etiquette then allowed the man to hit back. In his kitchen his favorite jest, habitual, was to say to a guest in front of their maid Elizabeth: "Lord knows, I do hate a nigger!" This brought huge guffaws from Elizabeth, and Peter was known widely as a hilarious crusty man, good to his toes. But I never thought this was funny, and I wanted my uncle to stop including me in this bullying niggerism, maybe go call a big white man a nigger.

While he was gone those two hours in the truck I figured on how mean an act this was to both me and the man stacking the fence poles. I never even looked his way. I was boiling mad and embarrassed and could not decide what the man, my uncle, *wanted* from this episode. Was he training me to be a leader of men? Was he squeezing this man, some special enemy, the last excruciating turn possible, by use of a mere skinny white boy, but superior kin, wearing his same name? I couldn't find an answer with a thing decent in it. I began hating Uncle Peter. When he came back I did not answer him when he wanted to tally my figure with the black man's. I said nothing at all. He looked at me in a slightly blurred way, his eyes like glowing knots in a pig's face, I thought. He had on his nice fedora but his face was spreading and reddening, almost as in a fiend movie. Too, I smelled something in the car as from an emergency room I'd been in when I was hit by that car, waking up to this smell.

"Wharoof? Did you ever answer? Didja gimme the number?"

"Have you been in an accident somewhere, Uncle Peter?"

"No. Let me tell you. I have no problem. I know you might've heard things. This"—he lifted out a pint bottle of vodka, Smirnoff—"is just another one of God's gifts, you understand? We can use it, or we can abuse it. It is a gift to man in his lonesomeness." To illustrate he lifted it, uncapped it, turned it up, and up came enormous bubbles from the lip as in an old water cooler seriously engaged. He took down more than half of the liquor. The man could drink in cowboy style, quite awesomely. I'd never heard a word about this talent before.

"I'm fessin' up. I'm a bad man. I was using you out here as an alibi for having a drink down the road there, so's your aunt wouldn't know. She has the wrong idea about it. But she knew I wouldn't drink with you along."

"You could drink right here in front of me. I wouldn't tell, anyway."

"Well. I'm glad to know it. It got to my conscience

and I came back to make my peace with you about it. Everything between you and me's on the up and up, pardner."

"You mean you didn't need me counting those poles at all?"

"Oh yes I did. It was a real job. It wasn't any Roosevelt make-work."

"Don't you consider that man over there has any feelings, what you said right in front of him?"

"What's wrong with shame, boy? Didn't you ever learn by it? You're tender and timid like your pop, you can't help it. But you're all right too."

"Anybody ever shame you real bad, Uncle Peter?"

He looked over, his jowls even redder and gone all dark and lax, gathered up by his furious eyes. "Maybe," he said. An honest answer would have been, had he come out with it all: "Once. And I killed him." I wonder how much of that event was in his mind as he looked at me sourly and said, "Maybe."

He feared my aunt, I knew it, and let me off at the house, driving off by himself while I gathered my stuff and waited for my folks to pick me up. I heard later that he did not return home for three weeks. For months, even a year, he would not drink, not touch a drop, then he would have a nip and disappear. Uncle Peter was a binge drinker. Still, I blamed my aunt, a fastidious and abrasive country woman with a previous marriage. It was a tragedy she could give him no children and I had to stand in as his line in the family. She blundered here and there, saying wrong and hurtful things, a hag of unnecessary truth at family gatherings—a comment about somebody's weight, somebody's hair, somebody's lack of backbone. She was always correcting and scolding when I visited and seemed to think this was the only conversation possible between the old and young, and would

have been baffled, I think, had you mentioned it as an unbearable lifetime habit. I blamed her for his drinking and
his insensitivity to blacks. He was doing it to show off to her,
that's what. He was drinking because he could not stand
being cruel.

The next time I saw him he had made me two fishing lures, painting them by hand in his shop. These he pre-
sented me along with a whole new Shakespeare casting reel
and rod. I'd never caught a fish on an artificial lure, and here
with the spring nearly on we had us a mission. His lakes were
full of big healthy bass. Records were broken every summer,
some of them by the grinning wives and children of his
customers, so obliged to Mister Peter, Squire of Lawrence
County. On his lands were ponds and creeks snapping with
fish almost foreign they were so remote from the roads and
highways. You would ramble and bump down through a far
pasture with black Angus in it, spy a stretch of water through
leaves, and as you came down to it you heard the fish in a
wild feeding so loud it could have been schoolchildren out
for a swim. I was trembling to go out with him to one of
these far ponds. It seemed forever before we could set out.
Uncle Peter had real business, always, and stayed in motion
constantly like a shark who is either moving or dead. Especially when he came out of a bender, paler and thinner, ashen
in the face almost like a deacon. He hurled himself into
penitential work. His clothes were plainer, like a sharecropper's more than the baron's, and it would be a few weeks
before you'd see the watch chain, the fedora, or the nice
boots—the cultured European scion among his vineyards,
almost.

I did not know there were women involved in these
benders, but there were. Some hussy in a motel in a bad
town. I'd imagine truly deplorable harlots of both races,

something so bad it took more than a bottle a day to maintain the illusion you were in the room with your own species. He went the whole hog and seemed unable to reroute the high lonesomes that came on him in other fashion. But had I known I'd have only cheered for his happiness against my aunt, whom I blamed for every misery in him.

At home my father meant very well, but he didn't know how to do things. He had no grace with utensils, tools, or equipment. We went fishing a great many times, never catching a thing after getting up at four and going long distances. I think of us now fishing with the wrong bait, at the wrong depth, at the wrong time. He could make money and drive (too slowly), but the processes of life eluded him. As a golfer he scored decently, but with an ugly chopping swing. He was near childlike with wonder when we traveled, and as to sports, girls, hobbies, and adventures my father remained somewhat of a wondering pupil throughout his life and I was left entirely to my own devices.

He had no envy of his wealthy brother's skills at all, on the other hand, only admiration. "Old Peter knows the *way* of things, doesn't he, son?" he'd cheer. It seemed perfectly all right that he himself was a dull and slow slob. I see my father and the men of his generation in their pinstripe suits and slicked-back hair, standing beside their new automobiles or another symbol of prosperity that was the occasion for the photograph, and these men I admire for accepting their own selves and their limits better, and without therapy. There's more peace in their looks, a more possessed handsomeness, even with the world war around them. You got what you saw more, I'd guess, and there was plainer language then, there had to be. My father loved his brother

and truly pitied him for having no son of his own. So he lent
me to him, often.

In the dullish but worthy ledger mark my father down
as no problem with temper, moodiness, or whiskey, a good
man of no unplesant surprises that way. He was sixty-five
years old before he caught a bass on a spinning reel with
artificial bait. He died before he had the first idea how to
work the remote control for the television.

At last Uncle Peter had the time to take me and himself out to a far pond, with a boat in the bed of the truck
and his radio dialed to his beloved Cardinals. We drove so
far the flora changed and the woods were darker, full of odd
lonesome long-legged fowl like sea birds. The temperature
dropped several degrees. It was much shadier back here
where nobody went. Uncle Peter told me he'd seen a snapping turtle the width of a washtub out in this pond. It was a
strange, ripe place, fed by springs, the water nearly as clear
as in Florida lakes.

He paddled while I threw a number of times and, in
my fury to have one on, messed up again and again with a
backlash, a miscast, and a wrap, my lure around a limb six
feet over the water next to a water moccasin who raised its
head and looked at me with low interest. I jerked the line, it
snapped, and the hand-painted lure of all Uncle Peter's effort
was marooned in the wood. I was a wretched fool, shaking
with a rush of bile.

"Take your time, little Pete. Easy does it, get a rhythm
for yourself."

I tied the other lure on. It was a bowed lure that
wobbled crazily on top of the water. I didn't think it had a
prayer and was still angry about losing the good one, which
looked exactly like a minnow. We were near the middle of

the pond, but the middle was covered with dead tree stumps and the water was clear a good ways down.

A big bass hit the plug right after it touched the water on my second cast. It never gave the plug a chance to be inept. It was the first fish I'd ever hooked on artificial bait, and it was huge. It moved the boat. My arms were yanked forward, then my shoulders, as the thing wanted to tear the rod out of my palms on the way to the pond bottom. I held up and felt suddenly a dead awful weight and no movement. The bass had got off and left me hooked on a log down there, I knew. What a grand fish. I felt just dreadful until I looked down into the water when the thrashing had cleared.

The fish was still on the plug in ten feet of water. It was smart to try to wrap the line around the submerged log, but it was still hooked itself and was just sitting there breathing from the gills like some big thing in an aquarium. My uncle was kneeling over the gunwale looking at the fish on the end of the line. His fedora fell in the water. He plucked it out and looked up at me in sympathy. I recall the situation drew a tender look from him such as I'd never quite seen.

"Too bad, little Pete. There she is, and there she'll stay. It's almost torture to be able to look at your big fish like that, ain't it? Doesn't seem fair."

Uncle Peter didn't seem to enjoy looking in the water. Something was wrong, besides this odd predicament.

"No. I'm going down for it. I'm going to get the fish."

"Why, boy, you can't do that."

"Just you watch. That fish is mine."

I took off all my clothes and was in such a hurry I felt embarrassed only at the last. I was small and thin and ashamed in front of Uncle Peter, but he had something like fear or awe on his face I didn't understand.

"That fish big as you are," he said in a foreign way. "That water deep and snakey."

But I did swim down, plucked up the fish by its jaws, and came back to throw it in the boat. The plug stayed down there, visible, very yellow, as a monument to my great boyhood enterprise, and I wonder what it looks like now, forty years later.

My uncle had the fish mounted for me. It stayed in our home until I began feeling sorry for it after Peter's death, and I gave it to a barber for his shop. The fish weighed about nine pounds, the biggest I'll ever catch.

I was not the same person to my uncle after that afternoon. I did not quite understand his regard of me until my father explained something very strange. Uncle Peter was much the country squire and master of many trades, but he could not swim and he had a deathly fear of deep water. He had wanted to join the navy, mainly for its white officers' suits, but they had got him near a deep harbor somewhere in Texas and he'd gone near psychotic. He seemed to expect great creatures to get out of the sea and come for him too and it was past reason, just one of those odd strands in the blood about which there can be no comment or change. Since then I've talked to several country people with the same fear, one of them an All-American linebacker. They don't know where it came from and don't much want to discuss it.

When television appeared I was much enamored of Howdy Doody. Some boys around the neighborhood and I began molding puppet heads from casts you could buy at the five-and-dime. You could have the heads of all the characters from the "Howdy" show in plaster of paris. Then you'd put a skirt with arms on it and commence the shows onstage. We wrote whole plays, very violent and full of weapons and traps, all in the spirit of nuclear disaster and Revelations, with Howdy, Flubadub, and Clarabelle. I couldn't get over my uncle's interest in the puppets when I brought them over and set up the show in his workshop.

The puppets seemed to worry him like a bouncing string would worry a cat. He looked at me as if I were magic, operating these little people and speaking for them. He had the stare of an intense confused infant. When I'd raise my eyes to him, he'd look a bit ashamed, as if he'd been seduced into thinking these toys were living creatures. He watched my mouth when I spoke in a falsetto for them.

I still don't know what the hell went on with him and the puppets, the way he watched them, then me. You'd have thought he was staring into a world he never even considered possible, somewhere on another planet; something he'd missed out on and was very anxious about. I noticed too that he would dress *up* a little for the puppet shows. Once he wore his fedora and a red necktie as well.

A number of years went by when I did not see my uncle much at all. These were my teen years when I was altogether a different person. He remained the same, and his ways killed him. I don't know if the dead man in his past urged him toward the final DT's and heart attack, nor will I ever know how much this crime dictated his life, but he seemed to be attempting to destroy himself in episode after episode when, as he would only say afterwards, the high lonesomes struck him.

The last curious scene when I recall him whole was the summer right after I turned thirteen. We were all around the beach of Bay St. Louis, Mississippi, where we'd gathered for a six-family reunion of my father's people. The gulf here was brown, fed by the Wolf and Jordan rivers. It provided groaning tables of oysters, shrimp, flounder, crabs, and mul-

let. Even the poor ate very well down here, where there were
Catholics, easy liquor and gambling, bingo, Cajuns, Sicilians,
and Slavs. By far it was the prettiest and most exotic of the
towns where any of the families lived, and my Uncle Max and
Aunt Ginny were very proud showing us around their great
comfortable home, with a screened porch running around
three sides where all the children slept for the cool breeze from
the bay. All over the house were long troughs of ice holding
giant watermelons and cantaloupes and great strawberries.
Something was cooking all the time. This was close to heaven,
and everybody knew it. You drifted off to sleep with the tales
of the aunts and uncles in your ears. What a bliss.

Most of us were on the beach or in the water when
Uncle Peter went most bizarre, although for this I do have
an interpretation that might be right. He had been watching me too intently, to the exclusion of others. He was too
around, I could feel his eyes close while I was in the water
swimming. He was enduring a sea change here at the sea,
which he was supposed to be deathly afraid of. I believe he
was turning more *urban,* or more cosmopolitan. He'd been
to a Big Dutchman convention in Chicago. Somebody had
convinced him to quit cigarettes, take up thin cigars, get a
massage, and wear an Italian hat, a borsalino hat, which he
now wore with sunglasses and an actual designed beach
towel, he and his wife sitting there in blue canvas director's
chairs. He had been dry for over a year, had lost weight, and
now looked somewhat like Versace, the Italian designer. If
this was our state's most European town, then by God Uncle
Peter would show the way, leading the charge with his Italian
hat high and his beach towel waving.

He was telling all of them how he was getting rid of
the bags under his eyes. He was going to take up tennis. He
had bought a Jaguar sedan, hunter green. Now on the beach

as he sat with the other uncles and my father, watching us kids swim, he seemed all prepared for a breakout into a new world, even if he couldn't swim, even in his pale country skin. Here he was in wild denial of his fear of the water. His wife, my aunt, seemed happier sitting there beside him. She'd been kinder lately, and I forgave her much. Maybe they had settled something at home.

I'll remember him there before the next moment, loved and honored and looking ahead to a breakout, on that little beach. He could be taken for a real man of the world, interested even in puppets, even in fine fabrics. You could see him—couldn't you?—reaching out to pet the world. Too long had he denied his force to the cosmos at large. Have me, have me, kindred, he might be calling. May my story be of use. I am meeting the ocean on its own terms. I am ready.

The New Orleans children were a foulmouthed group in general out there in the brown water of the bay. Their parents brought them over to vacation and many of the homes on the beach were owned by New Orleans natives. The kids were precocious and street-mouthed, sounding like Brooklynites really, right out of a juvenile delinquent movie. They had utter contempt for the local Crackers. The girls used rubes like me and my cousins to sharpen up their tongues. And they could astound and wither you if you let them get to you. They had that mist of Catholic voodoo around them too.

Some sunbrowned girl, maybe twelve, in a two-piece swimsuit, got nudged around while we were playing and started screaming at me.

"Hey Cracker, eat me!"

"What?"

"Knockin' me with ya foot! Climb on this!" She gave me the finger.

You see? Already deep into sin, weathered like a slut at a bingo table, from a neighborhood that smelled like whiskey on a hot bus exhaust. I guess Uncle Peter saw the distress in my face, although I was probably a year older than the girl. He had heard her too. He began raving at her across the sand and water, waving both arms. He was beside himself, shouting at her to "Never say those things! Never ever say those things to him!"

I looked at her, and here was another complicating thing. She had breasts and a cross dangling by a chain between them and was good-looking. Uncle Peter had come up to the waterline and was looking at her too, forcing his hooked finger down for emphasis, "Don't ever!" But she leaned back to mock this old man, and she confused him and broke his effect.

Another uncle called out for him to come back, I was old enough to take care of myself, there wasn't any real problem here. But Uncle Peter hurled around and said: "There *is* a problem. There *is*."

Then he left the beach by himself and we didn't see him the rest of the reunion. I saw my aunt sitting in their bedroom with her shoulders to me, her head forward, alone, and I understood there was huge tragedy in my uncle, regardless of anything she ever did.

A couple of the brothers went out on his trail. They said he began in a saloon near the seawall in Waveland.

Could it be as simple as that my uncle saw, in his nervous rage and unnatural mood, that girl calling me down the road to sin, and he exploded? That he saw my fate coming to me in my teens, as his had, when he killed the man? Or was he needing a drink so badly that none of this mattered? I don't know. After that bender he didn't much follow up on any great concern for me. Maybe he gave up on himself.

It took seven years more. My father came and got me at my apartment in the college town and told me about his death, in a hospital over in that county. My father had white hair by then, and I remember watching his head bowed over, his arm over the shoulders of his own, their mother, my grandmother, with her own white-haired head bowed in grief no mother should bear. My grandmother repeated over and over the true fact that Peter was always "doing things, always his projects, always moving places." His hands were busy, his feet were swift, his wife was bountifully well off, forever.

A man back in the '20s came to town and started a poker game. Men gathered and drank. Peter lost his money and started a fight. The man took a chair and repeatedly ground it into his face while Peter was on the floor. Peter went out into the town, found a pistol, came back, and shot the man. The brothers went about influencing the jury, noting that the victim was trash, an out-of-towner. The judge agreed. The victim was sentenced to remain dead. Peter was let go.

I've talked to my nephew about this. For years now I have dreamed I killed somebody. The body has been hidden, but certain people know I am guilty, and they show up and I know, deep within, what they are wanting, what this is all about. My nephew was nodding the whole while I was telling him this. He has dreamed this very thing, for years.